#2 Battle of the Bunheads

Look for these and other books
in the Bad News Ballet series:

Bad News Ballet

#2 Battle of the Bunheads

Jahnna N. Malcolm

AN
APPLE
PAPERBACK

SCHOLASTIC INC.
New York Toronto London Auckland Sydney

ISBN 0-590-41916-1

12 11 10 9 8 7 6 5 4 3 2 1   9/8 0 1 2 3 4/9

Printed in the U.S.A.   11

First Scholastic printing, April 1989

*FOR ROSAMOND HILLGARTNER
A MOM FOR ALL SEASONS*

Chapter One

"Mother, stop!" Mary Bubnik shouted, grabbing the dashboard of the car. "We're here."

Mrs. Bubnik slammed on the brakes and the green Volvo skidded on the icy street. Mary and her mother sat rigid, watching the buildings of downtown Deerfield whirr past. The car seemed to have a mind of its own, swerving first to the left, then to the right. Finally it gently came to rest against the curb.

"Mary, don't *ever* shout at me like that again!" Mrs. Bubnik rested her forehead against the wheel. "We could have been hurt."

"But, Mom, it's the Deerfield Academy of Dance!" Mary pointed at the white granite building with the

1

four big pillars that loomed in front of them. Then she grinned sheepishly at her mother. "I guess I got a little carried away."

"A *little*," her mother drawled in her southern accent. "I swear, one of these days you're going to give me a heart attack." Mrs. Bubnik sighed and ruffled her eleven-year-old daughter's hair. "But I understand how excited you must be. Today is a very special day."

Mary nodded her head so hard her blonde curls bounced. "Today I get to see Miss Jo and take a new ballet class and see my best friends." Mary's blue eyes suddenly clouded with worry. "Do you think they'll have changed?"

"I don't see why," Mrs. Bubnik said, patting her daughter on the knee. "It's barely been a month since you've seen them."

Mary remembered the first time she had met the gang. It was the day she auditioned for the Deerfield Academy of Dance's holiday production of *The Nutcracker*. Having just moved to Ohio, she was feeling pretty lonely. Meeting her four friends had changed everything. Mary Bubnik smiled as she thought of them. McGee, Gwen, Zan and Rocky — each very different and very special.

Mrs. Bubnik maneuvered the car away from the curb and then slowly moved down the street toward the big stone building.

"Boy, Mom, it's really starting to snow!" Mary Bubnik leaned forward and peered through the windshield. Big white flakes flew through the air and turned to ice as they hit the cold glass. "I can hardly see."

"Maybe this will help." Mrs. Bubnik turned a knob and the windshield wipers sprang to life. "There. Now, if we could just get the heater to work, everything would be just fine." Mrs. Bubnik pounded hard on the cracked dashboard of the old Volvo. "It would choose the middle of a snowstorm to call it quits." She muttered under her breath, "Maybe we should think about buying another car."

Mary's eyes widened. "You can't get rid of Mr. Toad! He's part of the family." Her parents had bought the dark green car eleven years ago, just after Mary had been born. After the divorce, it had been one of the few things she and her mother had taken with them to Ohio.

"I'll give him one more chance." Mrs. Bubnik gave the dashboard a solid whack and the heater whirred back to life. Mary and her mother both laughed.

As the windshield defogged, Mary recognized a figure off to their right. "Mom, it's Zan!" Mary pointed to a tall black girl slowly making her way along the frozen sidewalk. She was wearing a lavender beret and matching gloves. Her head was buried in the book she was reading, and with one hand she kept brushing away the snowflakes as they hit the page. Zan didn't seem to notice any of the people who were swerving to avoid bumping into her. Mary rolled down her window and shouted, "Well, if it isn't Suzannah Reed, old bookworm herself!"

Zan lifted her head and blinked, her big brown eyes staring in confusion at the people around her.

"Yoo-hoo! Zan! Over here." Mary leaned out the window and waved both hands up and down frantically.

When Zan spotted Mary, her face spread into a glowing smile. She tucked her book under one arm and hurried toward the car.

Mary pulled her head back, quickly kissed her mother on the cheek, then threw open the car door and hopped onto the sidewalk. "Bye, Mom. I've got to go."

"Mary Bubnik, you just hold your horses!" Her mother's southern accent twanged in the air. "You forgot your ballet slippers."

Mary groaned. "Mom, you know they're too big for me." She had left them behind on purpose, and was planning to take ballet class in her stocking feet.

"Put these on." Mrs. Bubnik handed her daughter a pair of thick orange knee socks. "They should make your shoes fit just fine."

"Do you really think so?" Mary stuffed the socks in her coat pocket. Her feet already looked huge in her big floppy shoes. With the bright orange knee socks she knew they'd look gigantic.

"I'm sure of it." Mrs. Bubnik pulled away from the curb and shouted, "And if they're still too big, stuff a little Kleenex in the toes."

"Kleenex!" Mary shook her head. She watched her mother's car sputter and cough its way down the street. Mrs. Bubnik honked loudly as she passed Zan.

Mary ran to greet her friend with a huge hug. "Gee, Zan," she said, smiling at her, "I sure missed you."

Although both Zan and Mary were in the fifth grade, Zan was a whole foot taller. But that was nothing new for Zan. She was the tallest girl in all of Stewart Elementary School, sixth-graders included. The fact that she was so thin made her look even taller.

"I missed you, too," Zan said in her soft voice. "I thought Christmas vacation would never end. I finished reading all of my library books in the very first week."

Zan loved reading more than anything. She liked poetry and romance, but her favorite books were about the adventures of Tiffany Truenote, teen detective. Tiffany was outgoing and popular, and Zan secretly wished she could be just like her.

"Well, I didn't read a single book," Mary said with a giggle. "But Mom and I did see about a dozen

5

movies. And you'll be happy to know that I practiced my ballet steps. I want to be able to keep up with you guys."

The rest of the gang had all taken ballet lessons before joining the Deerfield Academy of Dance. Mary Bubnik was the only one who hadn't. But she had studied three years of tap and baton twirling in El Reno, Oklahoma.

Zan patted Mary on the arm. "I don't think you have to worry about keeping up. None of us is really any good."

"Speak for yourself," a voice growled from behind them.

Mary spun around to see a slender girl leaning against a parking sign. She was wearing a red satin jacket and a huge grin. Her thick mane of dark curly hair seemed to explode out of her head every which way. Printed on the back of her jacket in silver lettering was her name.

"Rocky!" Mary cried happily. She leaped forward and wrapped her arms around the other girl.

"Look out!" Rochelle Garcia yelled, but it was too late. Mary's exuberant hug knocked them both off balance. They clung to each other, their feet slipping and sliding, until they hit the ground with a loud *thud.*

"Are you two all right?" Zan raced to help them, but her feet hit the same patch of ice. Before she knew what was happening she had landed in a heap on top of them.

"Wow!" Rocky said. "That's some hello."

"Gosh, I am so sorry!" Mary Bubnik tried to stand up. Her feet kept slipping out from under her, and she collapsed back onto Rocky again.

"It's a good thing I didn't want to be a dancer," Rocky said, shoving Mary Bubnik off her lap. "Otherwise my career would be over. I think you flattened my foot."

"Oh, no!" Mary Bubnik managed to grab the parking sign and pull herself to her feet. "That's terrible."

"That's OK," Rocky grinned. "I've got another one." She scrambled to her feet, then offered her hand to Zan and pulled her up beside her.

Zan started giggling. "If it took us this long to stand up, I don't think we'll learn to dance."

"Who cares?" Rocky shrugged. "Remember, we're only taking this class so we can see each other."

"That's right," Mary said, still clinging to the parking sign. "And aren't we supposed to meet McGee and Gwen about now?"

Rocky checked her watch. "Our meeting was set for exactly fourteen hundred hours."

Mary Bubnik looked confused. "What time is that?"

"That's military talk for two o'clock." Rocky grinned. "My dad talks like that all the time. It's hard to break the habit."

Rocky's father was a sergeant in the Air Force. The Garcias lived at nearby Curtiss-Dobbs Air Force Base and Sgt. Garcia ran his family like a miniature army.

"According to my watch," Zan said in her soft voice, "we're five minutes late."

"What are we waiting for?" Rocky threw her long black scarf over her shoulder. "Come on!"

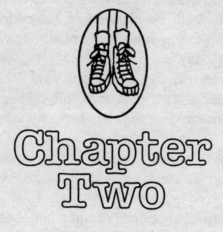

Chapter Two

The three friends linked arms and half-ran, half-skidded across the icy street. Once they were safely across, they paused in front of a small restaurant wedged between two tall buildings. A friendly red and white sign hung above the entrance.

"Here it is!" Zan announced. "Hi Lo's Pizza and Chinese Food To Go."

A bell above the glass door tinkled as they stepped into the tiny place. There was one booth against the back wall. Six round stools, covered in faded red leather, lined a curved counter. An old Chinese man was seated behind the counter. He was reading a newspaper, his wire-rim glasses resting firmly on the tip of his nose.

9

"Hi, Hi!" they sang out together.

Mr. Hi Lo looked up from his paper, and his face creased into hundreds of tiny wrinkles as he smiled. "Well, well, well!" He clapped his hands together in delight. "You three have brought sun into an otherwise dreary day."

"That's an awfully nice thing to say," Mary Bubnik said, giggling. The girls took off their coats and hung them on the wooden rack standing by the door.

"Are we the first to arrive?" Rocky asked as they hopped on to the worn leather stools circling the counter.

"We were all supposed to meet here before ballet class," Zan explained.

"Oh?" Mr. Lo raised a curious eyebrow. "So you girls have decided to continue your dancing lessons, have you?"

"We figured we had to," Mary explained, shoving off from the counter and letting her stool spin in a circle. "Otherwise, we figured we'd never see each other again."

All of the girls attended different schools around Deerfield. Zan's school was close to downtown, within walking distance of her parents' apartment. Mary attended Glenwood Elementary on the outskirts of the city, while Rocky was in the sixth grade at the school on the Air Force base. They had each convinced their mothers to let them take lessons together at the academy downtown.

"What can I get you while you're waiting for McGee and Gwen?" the old man asked as he set paper placemats in front of them. "The Hi Lo special is extremely good today."

"What's the special?" Rocky asked.

Hi pointed to the menu tacked above the grill.

"Hot-Cha-Cha Chocolate," Rocky read out loud. "The chocolate sounds good but what's the 'Hot-Cha-Cha' part?"

"Ah!" Mr. Lo's eyes twinkled. "That's my secret ingredient."

The three girls glanced at each other in silence. Finally Mary spoke up. "I don't think we'll have the special today, Hi," she said, "I mean, we're going to have to dance and all."

What she didn't say was that Hi Lo's secret ingredients could be pretty weird at times. They might be wonderful, like raspberry jam on ice cream, but they could also be very peculiar, like peanut butter and bananas in a chocolate shake. With Hi Lo, you never could tell.

Mr. Lo shrugged his shoulders good-naturedly. "OK. You could be missing the special of the century."

Thwack!

Something exploded against the front window of

the restaurant and the girls all screamed.

"What's going on?" Mr. Lo shouted.

A short girl, with long chestnut braids sticking out from under a wool stocking cap, charged into the restaurant.

"Look out!" she yelled. "We're under attack!" She held a big chunk of snow in her mittened hands as she huddled by the door.

"It's McGee!" Mary Bubnik cried, just as another white ball of snow exploded against the glass.

Rocky leaped off her stool and raced to McGee's side. "Give me some of that," she said. Without taking her eyes off her attackers, Kathryn McGee handed Rocky some of the snow.

"Who do you think it is?" Rocky asked as she packed the snow into a hard ball.

"I'm not sure," McGee muttered. "But I have an idea."

Rocky leaped up and flung open the door. Taking aim, she threw as hard as she could at a group of kids clustered behind a car in front of the restaurant. One of them was wearing a blue coat, and the snowball exploded in a puff of white against it.

"Bull's-eye!" McGee cried.

"That ought to hold 'em!" Rocky raised one of her hands. "Give me five!"

McGee slapped her mittened hand against Rocky's. Then the two girls turned to face the others, who sat in stunned silence.

"Good to see you guys," McGee said. She flashed a grin and took off her stocking cap. Her freckled cheeks were rosy pink from the cold, and snowflakes clung to the lashes of her bright green eyes.

"That was an amazing entrance!" Hi Lo hurried to the front window and checked the glass. "Fortunately, nothing is broken. Your attackers seem to have completely disappeared."

"I hope so." McGee hopped onto the nearest stool. "How ya doin', Hi?"

"I am quite well, thank you." Mr. Lo smiled. "And how is your hockey team? Still winning?"

McGee was the athlete of the bunch and fiercely proud of being the first girl member of her town's ice hockey team, the Fairview Express. She nodded. "Yep, we're ten and oh. But we have to face the Ice Warriors this week, and they're really hot."

"Does your coach still feel OK about your ballet lessons?" Mary Bubnik asked.

"Yeah, he's cool." When McGee had first joined the cast of *The Nutcracker,* she worried that her coach and teammates would make fun of her. At first she tried to keep it a secret, but in the end they all found out about it. To her surprise, the coach thought her ballet lessons were a good idea. He had even brought some of her teammates to see the performance.

"How about your team?" Rocky added. "Anybody called you a sissy lately?"

"Nope." McGee giggled. "And here's the really weird part. Jason, our goalie, has been talking about signing up for ballet lessons, and that's made a few other guys interested, too."

"You're kidding." Zan was amazed. When she had met McGee's team, they all looked like big hulking sixth-graders who wouldn't be caught dead in a dance class.

"I think our rat dance really impressed them," McGee said, referring to the parts they had played in *The Nutcracker.*

"It certainly impressed me." Mr. Lo grinned. "I especially liked the way you came down the aisle and scared the audience half to death."

The girls all smiled, remembering the performance. They had been locked out of the theatre on opening night, and the only way for them to get to the stage was through the auditorium. They had scurried down the aisles, making scary faces at people along the way. Luckily, their entrance was a big hit with the audience who applauded loudly at the end.

"Everything was great about the ballet," Mary Bubnik said with a sigh, "except for our awful costumes."

"That's for sure," Rocky agreed. "They didn't fit anybody."

Zan nodded. "Big lumpy things that made us all look terrible."

"And remember how Gwen called them fat suits?" Mary Bubnik said.

"Where is Gwen, anyway?" Zan asked McGee. "I thought you two were coming together."

"Geez Louise!" McGee shouted, nearly falling off her stool. "I left her outside."

"How could you do that?" Mary Bubnik asked.

"Just as Mrs. Hays dropped us off, Gwen got into some sort of argument with her. Then someone started throwing snowballs at us, and I said I'd go for help." McGee zipped up her vest. "She's still out there hiding. I'd better go get her."

Then suddenly a blast of cold air filled the room as a plump girl with short, straight red hair stumbled in and shouted, "I'm blind!"

"Gwen, are you OK?" McGee asked.

Gwendolyn Hays, clad in a green wool coat and soggy gloves, stood with her arms outstretched. Her glasses had completely fogged up when she hit the warm air of Hi Lo's restaurant.

"I'm blind and frozen." Gwen walked stiffly up to the counter and took off her gloves. Then she grabbed a napkin from a metal canister and wiped her glasses.

"Gosh, it looks like they got you." Mary Bubnik pointed to the thick patches of snow clinging to her shoulders and back.

Gwen put on her glasses and focused her green eyes in Mary's direction. "They got me," she admitted with quiet dignity, "but not anywhere that hurt." Gwen held up her canvas dance bag. "I used this as a shield."

The blue bag was caked with snow. The toe shoes painted on the side were barely visible.

"Good thinking." Rocky patted Gwen on the back.

"Yeah," Gwen said with a grin. "I knew this bag would finally come in handy some day."

"But isn't that for carrying your ballet slippers and clothes?" Mr. Lo asked.

"That's what my mother thinks," Gwen said. "You see, she ordered it from *Dance Magazine* because — " Gwen raised her voice to imitate her mother. " 'All of the really famous ballerinas in New York City use these.' "

It was very important to Gwen's mother that her daughter be in style and popular. Mrs. Hays was tall, thin, and beautiful. She had perfect manners, hosted many "lovely" parties, and always did the "right" thing. Mrs. Hays was certain that, with a little guidance, Gwendolyn would turn out to be just like her.

Gwen had her doubts. At the age of twelve, she was still the complete opposite of her mother — short, plump, and nearsighted.

"If you don't carry ballet clothes in there," Mr. Lo asked, "what makes it so full?"

Gwen set her blue canvas bag on the counter and it made a loud clinking sound. "Snacks. And other important items, like books and stuff." A worried look crossed her face. "I hope the food didn't get hurt by the snowballs."

She unzipped the bag and the girls peered inside. A bag of corn chips, several granola bars, and two cans of diet soda could be seen. There were also three library books, several magazines, and a small Walkman.

Thwack!

Another snowball exploded in a puff of white against the door.

"Hey, it's those kids again!" Rocky threw open the glass door and charged out onto the sidewalk. The rest of the girls hopped off their stools and raced to join her.

Outside they glimpsed three figures scurrying across the street. At the foot of the snow-covered steps leading up to Hillberry Hall, their attackers spun around to face the girls.

A pretty dark-haired girl in a black coat crossed her arms and stared hard in their direction. Her hair was pulled into a tight bun on top of her head. Beside her stood a slim blonde, dressed in an identical black wool coat and wearing her hair in an identical bun. Next to them was a smaller girl with mousy features, clutching an armful of snowballs to her blue coat. She sported the same hairdo.

A slow smile crept across the lips of the brunette, and the gang all groaned in dismay. "Oh, no! It's the Bunheads!"

17

Chapter Three

"We can't be in the same class as the Bunheads," McGee moaned as they made their way up the steps of Hillberry Hall. "That would be awful!"

"It'd be torture!" Rocky kicked at one of the big stone pillars when they reached the top.

"Just like the rehearsals for *The Nutcracker*," Mary Bubnik added, "when they made fun of us and were so mean."

All during rehearsals for *The Nutcracker*, Courtney Clay and her friends had done everything they could to make the gang look bad. The other girls' dance clothes were just perfect. They always wore their hair in tight buns on top of their heads. Rocky

18

had called them "Bunheads" one day and the name just stuck.

"Let's talk to Miss Delacorte," Zan said, swinging open the door to the big stone building. "Because I just can't imagine taking another class with those girls. It would be too, too terrible."

Zan was the only one of the five who'd actually taken classes at the academy before. She had spent the previous summer in ballet class with Courtney Clay and her friends. They were very mean to her, teasing her about her height and shyness. She most definitely didn't want that to happen again.

Gwen slung her dance bag over her shoulder. "They can just move us to another class."

"Better yet," Rocky giggled, "they can move the Bunheads!"

"Yeah!" They made their way to the third floor, where the Deerfield Academy of Dance was located. Miss Natalya Delacorte, the Russian receptionist, was seated behind the oak desk just inside the door. She was dressed all in gray except for a bright red turban that perched cheerily on her head. "Well, if it isn't the lee-tle mice from our ballet. How was your holiday?"

"Just great!" Rocky said as they all clustered around the desk. "But..." She paused, trying to figure out what to say next.

"But what?" Miss Delacorte folded her long, thin fingers in front of her.

19

"We have this teensy problem," Gwen explained.

"That's right," Mary Bubnik added. "You see, it's those Bun — "

Rocky silenced Mary with a swift jab in the side, and McGee quickly said, "It's about our dance class."

"Is there another one that we could possibly join?" Zan asked.

"Whatever for?" Miss Delacorte trilled. "This Saturday class is just perfect for you girls. Your teacher is Annie Springer, and she is absolutely lovely."

"We still want to change," Gwen persisted.

"For personal reasons," Zan said, looking mysterious.

"Yeah." Rocky wiggled her eyebrows meaningfully. "It's for personal reasons."

Miss Delacorte pursed her lips in thought. "I suppose you could change to the Wednesday evening class."

McGee shook her head. "It has to be on Saturday."

"I'm sorry, girls." Miss Delacorte held her arms out in a gesture of helplessness. "The fact of the matter is, on Saturday there is only one class suitable for girls your age." She gestured toward the dressing room at the far end of the reception area. "Now, hurry. You don't want to be late for your first class of the year."

The gang went into a huddle near the couch.

Piano music sounding from behind several doors signified that dance classes were in progress.

"What do we do now?" Zan whispered.

McGee shrugged. "We take the class."

"With the Bunheads?" Gwen groaned.

Rocky nodded miserably. "We don't have any other choice."

"Not if we want to stay together," Zan added.

"Which is the most important thing of all," Mary Bubnik said earnestly. She looked at the others, who nodded their heads in agreement.

Finally Gwen sighed, "I guess we should just take the class with the Bunheads and try our best to get along."

"And if they're nice to us," Rocky said, "we'll be nice to them."

"Right!"

The five girls shuffled into the curtained dressing room and were immediately greeted by Alice Wescott, the thin fourth-grader with the high-pitched voice. "The Rats are back," she called over her shoulder to Courtney Clay, who was seated at the makeup table.

"So much for being nice," Gwen muttered under her breath.

Courtney Clay wrinkled her nose at the newcomers. "What are you doing here?"

"You've got three guesses," Rocky shot back, "and the first two don't count."

"Very funny," Courtney sniffed.

Page Tuttle, a thin, delicate blonde seated beside Courtney said, "Why did you come back? This academy is for serious dancers *only.*"

Of all the Bunheads, Page Tuttle was the most fashion-conscious. She had a different leotard for every day of the week and always had a copy of *Dance Magazine* tucked in her dance bag.

"Well, if you don't like it," McGee retorted, "you can just leave."

Courtney stood up, her nostrils flaring angrily. "Why should *we* leave? We were here first!"

"The way you're acting," Zan said, dropping her dance clothes on the nearest bench, "you'd think you owned the studio."

"She does, practically." Alice Wescott put her hands on her hips. "I mean, her mother *is* on the board of directors."

Rocky shrugged. "Big deal."

"It's a *very* big deal," Page Tuttle said. "The board of directors determines everything that happens in the ballet company."

"So who cares?" Gwen snapped. "We're just here to take a dumb class."

"Dumb?" Courtney suddenly walked to the blackboard that hung against the wall of the dressing room. It was covered with notices to the company. "We'll see who's dumb!" She picked up a piece of chalk and drew a line down the center of the dress-

22

ing room. The chalk squeaked against the hard-wood floor.

"What'd you do that for?" Mary Bubnik asked, covering her ears against the awful noise.

"That's your side of the room," Courtney said smugly. She gestured with the chalk to the half of the dressing room that held the row of metal lockers and a lone coatrack. "The *dumb* side." She pointed to where she had been sitting. "And this is *ours.* As long as you stay on your side and don't bother us, we'll get along just fine." She set the chalk back on its tray and dusted off her hands with a satisfied clap.

"You've got to be kidding," McGee exploded.

"That is absolutely unfair," Zan complained. "You have the dressing table, the chairs, and the full-length mirror."

"The mirror?" Gwen repeated with a gasp. "Oh, no!" The tall free-standing mirror was the only thing in the room that she could hide behind to change clothes. Not even her own mother ever saw her get dressed. The thought of having to undress out in the open in front of strangers sent her into a complete panic.

"It's obvious none of you care about how you look or dress." Page Tuttle pointed at McGee, who had just pulled on her faded pink tights with a huge run up one leg. "Why do you need a mirror?"

"To keep from looking at you!" Gwen cried out.

Before anyone could stop her, she dashed across the line, grabbed the mirror and wheeled it toward the gang's side of the room. "Now it's ours!"

"No, you don't!" Alice Wescott lunged forward to stop her.

Rocky stepped in front of Alice. "Touch that mirror and you'll be sorry. Nobody likes a ballerina with a broken leg."

Alice turned white as a sheet. She backed away from Rocky slowly, muttering, "You don't have to get nasty."

"Get a load of her." Rocky pointed at Alice with her thumb. "Who's the one who was throwing snowballs?"

Zan pointed to the chairs and benches lining the Bunhead's side of the room. "What I want to know is, where are we supposed to sit?"

"You can sit on the floor for all I care," Courtney said, as she peered coolly at her reflection in the mirror. She carefully applied a hint of blusher to each cheek and added, "But don't cross that line."

McGee grabbed the end of a wooden bench and yanked it over to their side.

"You give us back that bench!" Page ordered.

Rocky and McGee stood side by side at the edge of the line. "Come and get it!"

"This is just not nice," Mary Bubnik's voice started to quiver. "We should all try to be friends. We're going to be in this class together for the rest of the year."

"Rest of the year?" Courtney laughed. "You won't last for the rest of the month."

"Want to bet?" Rocky challenged.

At that moment the curtain was thrown back, and Miss Delacorte peeked into the dressing room.

"Ah, I see you girls have been do-ink some re-modeling, yes?" She smiled at the two groups, who glared silently at each other. "It looks much better this way."

"Thank you, Miss Delacorte," Courtney said in a sweet voice. She looked Rocky straight in the eye and added, "We *like* it this way."

"Courtney, my dear, would you mind calling roll today?" Miss Delacorte asked. "Annie Springer is in a meeting and will be a little late."

"Certainly, Miss Delacorte, I'd be delighted to help," Courtney purred, smiling smugly at the gang.

As soon as Miss Delacorte left the dressing room, Courtney announced to her friends, "I know what the meeting's all about."

"Oooh, tell us!" Page Tuttle squealed, tugging on Courtney's arm.

"I can't. It's a *very* big secret." Courtney stretched her leg into a high arabesque behind her. She waited as several other girls entered the dressing room and began to change into their leotards and tights. Then she said loudly, "Mother and the board of directors have been working on this project since before Christmas."

McGee and the others stood quietly, pretending not to listen. But every part of their bodies was tuned into hearing the big secret.

"I tell you all of my most important secrets," Page said in a pouty voice. "Like when my parents divorced and when my brother had to be sent to military school."

"Oh, Page, you know what I mean!" Courtney raised up on her toe shoes and carefully *bourréed* in tiny steps across the floor. "My secret is much bigger than Deerfield, Ohio. It'll be big news all over the country. Even Daddy is involved in this one, and he usually couldn't care less about ballet, or any of Mother's projects."

"I still don't understand why you can't tell me," Page said, her pale blue eyes glistening with hurt. "I am your best friend."

Courtney, who was still *en pointe,* twirled in a tiny circle. "I'm afraid *they* might be listening." She fluttered one delicate hand in the direction of the gang, who stood frozen in a listening position.

Rocky straightened up and, pulling her wild hair into a side ponytail, said, "We couldn't care less about your silly secrets."

"Yeah, we have a dance class to take," McGee

said as she and the others followed Rocky across the chalk line to the curtained door.

"And we want to get used to the studio," Gwen added. "Since we're going to be here a long, *long* time."

Courtney's voice sliced through the air after them. "Not if I can help it!"

Chapter Four

Several girls were already in the ballet studio limbering up, when the gang entered the big light-filled room. One whole wall was covered with mirrors and rows of ballet *barres* lined the other. Mrs. Bruce, the accompanist, was already in her seat at the piano, shuffling through her sheet music.

The gang took their positions at the end of the room, as far from the piano and teacher as possible. They didn't want to seem too enthusiastic about taking ballet lessons. After all, they were only taking the class to be together.

Page and Alice threw back the door to the studio and Courtney swept in, holding the roll book like a badge of office. She walked up to the piano and nodded at the accompanist.

"Hello, Mrs. Bruce, it's good to see you again."

Mrs. Bruce looked up from her music with a vague smile.

"Class." Courtney clapped her hands together. "May I have your attention, please?"

Several girls whispering by the mirrors turned and focused their attention on her curiously.

"I have been asked to call roll and start the class for today," Courtney announced in a clear, precise voice.

"Get a load of her," Gwen whispered. "She acts like she's the teacher."

"Several of you look new to the Academy," Courtney continued, "so I'd like to welcome you."

"Give me a break," Rocky groaned.

Courtney shot Rocky a warning look. "The Academy is for serious ballerinas, but every now and then some misfits get in." Her lips narrowed into a thin, tight smile. "But they always get weeded out."

As she called the roll, Courtney kept her eyes focused on the gang. She made a big deal about calling McGee by her proper name, Kathryn, which made McGee grind her teeth. When she called Rocky, Rochelle, Rocky didn't even answer. Courtney quickly went on through the rest of the class.

"Now everyone will please line up at the *barre*,"

Courtney announced. "We will begin with *pliés*."
She made a grand gesture to Mrs. Bruce to begin
to play. The plump old lady completely missed the
signal. She was too busy rifling through her huge
leather bag for a tissue.

McGee was the first to get the giggles. She tried
to stifle them behind her hand, but that only made
them more obvious. Courtney's eyes flashed angrily
and she ordered, "Silence!" Mrs. Bruce, who had
finally found a Kleenex, answered her with a loud
honk.

Gwen and Rocky laughed out loud. Zan and Mary
Bubnik couldn't control themselves and collapsed
into titters. Soon all of the girls on their side of the
studio were in hysterics.

Courtney slammed the roll book down on the
piano, causing a startled Mrs. Bruce to toss her
Kleenex up in the air in fright. That set off a whole
new eruption of laughter.

"Silence, right this minute!" Courtney shouted.
Her voice could hardly be heard above the din. Even
Page, Alice, and a few other Bunheads were
snickering.

Suddenly, the studio door opened, and a beautiful, dark-haired girl glided into the room. Everyone
fell silent at the sight of her. She wore a long-sleeved
black leotard with a low-cut back. The matching
black nylon dance skirt that was wrapped around

her waist swirled gracefully as she walked. Her hair was parted in the middle and swept into a coil at the nape of her neck.

"Why, it's the Sugar Plum Fairy!" Mary Bubnik cried, recognizing the dancer from her role in the holiday production of *The Nutcracker.* "Annie Springer."

The lovely ballerina turned to Mary and smiled, revealing a tiny dimple in her cheek. "That's right. How sweet of you to remember."

Mary Bubnik blushed a deep red. "Who could forget you?"

McGee, Gwen, and Rocky pressed forward to meet the ballerina. Zan, who was usually shy, heard herself gush, "You were perfectly wonderful!"

Rocky nodded. "The best."

"Why, thank you." The dancer tilted her head slightly. "You five look very familiar to me."

"We were with you in *The Nutcracker,*" Gwen announced proudly.

Miss Springer put one delicate finger to her lips and studied the girls. "What parts did you dance?"

Suddenly they all felt tongue-tied. None of them wanted to be the one to tell their lovely new teacher what they had actually played. It was too embarrassing.

Courtney did it for them. "They played the lowly rats."

"Oh, yes." Annie Springer raised a knowing eyebrow. "You were certainly a big hit with the audience."

"Thanks, Miss Springer," Mary Bubnik murmured.

"Well, since we've danced together," the slender brunette said, "please, call me Annie."

"The audience really seemed to like our dance, too," Page Tuttle burst in. She gestured grandly to the Bunheads.

Annie turned to look at the other girls. "And what did you dance?"

Page's face fell. Alice Wescott piped up in her high, nasal voice, "We were the flowers."

"Oh, of course, I'm sorry." Annie graced them with a smile, then faced the room and clapped her hands together. "Well, we should really get started. I have a lot to cover today. Let's begin with roll call."

"I've already done that," Courtney said, strutting up to join the teacher at the front of the class. When Miss Springer cocked her head in confusion, Courtney explained, "I was asked to by Miss Delacorte. You see, I'm Courtney Clay."

Courtney waited patiently for her to be impressed. Annie simply nodded pleasantly. Courtney hinted, "My mother is on the board of directors."

"Oh, Cornelia Clay?"

Courtney nodded. She smiled smugly out at the

roomful of girls, satisified that she had regained her proper position.

"Well, I've just been meeting with your mother and the rest of the company." Annie perched lightly on a bench by the window and said, "Gather 'round, everyone. I have some terrific news."

"Great," Gwen whispered to Rocky. "The more time she kills on this stuff, the less time we'll have to spend doing those awful warm-ups."

"Let's sit close," Zan said, hurrying to grab a spot on the floor right in front of the ballerina.

"I still can't believe we have the Sugar Plum Fairy for our very own teacher," Mary Bubnik replied, her voice a little breathless with excitement.

Annie delicately folded her hands in her lap as she waited for the class to get comfortable. Then she smiled and announced, "The International Ballet is coming to America!"

Most of the class responded with a loud "Oooh!" Rocky and McGee and a few of the others just stared blankly back at their teacher.

Mary Bubnik shyly raised her hand. "Excuse me for asking, but what's the International Ballet?"

Page Tuttle leaned over to Courtney and hissed, loud enough for the whole class to hear, "What would a hick from Oklahoma know?"

Mary's eyes clouded with hurt as Courtney and her friends snickered. Mary quickly recovered, say-

33

ing, "I know it's a dumb question, but I'm kind of new to this whole ballet thing."

"It's not a dumb question at all," Annie reassured Mary. "The International Ballet is one of the finest ballet companies in the world. They're from Paris, France."

"Does that mean they speak French?" Mary asked, blinking her big blue eyes.

"Well, of course, they speak French," Courtney spoke up. "What did you think — Russian?"

Annie shot Courtney a reprimanding look. "Some of the dancers do speak Russian, Mary. And Italian and German and, of course, French. That's what makes them so very special. They're the best dancers from all around the world."

"And they're coming to America," Zan sighed.

Annie nodded. "Not only are they coming to the United States, but they will be giving a performance here in Deerfield!"

The class applauded happily.

"Whatever for?" Gwen wondered out loud. When the class turned to stare at her, she shrugged and said, "I mean, let's face it, Deerfield is not the most exciting place in the world."

"Well, their director is an old friend of Mr. Anton and Miss Jo, our company directors," Annie explained. "They all toured together in their younger days."

Page Tuttle raised her hand. "Didn't Mr. Anton used to be the dance partner for their prima ballerina, Alexandra Petrovna?"

"Alexandra Petrovna!" Zan sat straight up. "I've heard of her!"

"Everyone has," Annie said, her eyes glowing brightly. "She is the best ballerina alive today." Her voice grew low and hushed. "I saw her dance a few years ago, and I'll never forget it. It gives me chills just thinking about it."

This time Zan raised her hand. "I remember reading that she escaped from Romania on a train and it was really terrifying."

"That's right," Annie replied with a nod. "She hid in a suitcase."

"What is she, a midget?" McGee asked.

"No, no!" Annie laughed. "It was really more of a steamer trunk than a suitcase. They're a lot larger. But *this* suitcase had a removable back, just big enough to hide a person."

Gwen shook her head in wonder. "Just the same, I don't think I could get my head in a suitcase, let alone my whole body."

"That's the truth," Page whispered to Courtney. Gwen shot them her best dirty look.

"She nearly got caught at the border because the guards were inspecting everyone's luggage," Zan said, continuing the tale. "Luckily, a friend riding in the next compartment pretended to get terribly sick and in the confusion, the guards skipped the bag she was hiding in. It saved Alexandra Petrovna's life."

"That is amazing," Mary Bubnik said to Zan, shaking her head with awe.

Zan nodded. "It is, isn't it."

"No, no, I mean that you can know all that stuff."

"I read about it in a book called *Great Escapes.*"

Mary Bubnik turned to the rest of the girls and announced proudly, "Zan is like a walking encyclopedia. She knows everything. Go ahead, ask her something."

Before Zan could protest, Page Tuttle sang out, "What is the role Alexandra Petrovna is most famous for?"

"I don't know." Zan looked confused. "The book I read wasn't about ballet."

"Well, *everybody* knows that her *Giselle* is the best ever," Courtney replied smugly.

"I cried when I saw her dance it," Annie said softly. "Which brings me to the next, and most important, part of my announcement."

An excited murmur ran around the room as the girls crowded in closer.

"Alexandra Petrovna will be dancing *Giselle* here for one performance only. The board has decided that one lucky student from this academy will be chosen to present a bouquet of roses to her at the curtain call."

"Oh, I wish it were me!" Mary Bubnik cried. McGee never would have admitted it out loud, but she secretly hoped she might be picked, too. Gwen, Rocky, and Zan were all feeling the same way.

"This is a great honor and privilege," Annie reminded them. "And a bit of a problem. We spent the better part of that meeting trying to decide how to pick our flower bearer."

"Miss Springer?" Courtney raised her hand again. "My mother told me that the older dancers will get to take a master class with Miss Petrovna."

"That's right," the ballerina agreed. "And the younger students are still too little to appreciate the honor. So . . ."

Mary Bubnik held her breath.

"We decided the flower bearer should come from the fifth and sixth grade classes."

A cheer went up from the girls in the room. Annie held up her hand. "Those are the Monday, Wednesday, and Saturday classes."

"Three classes." McGee added them up. "Hey, that gives us a fighting chance."

Zan squeezed Mary Bubnik's hand. "Wouldn't it be great if it were one of us?"

"Two girls from each class will be nominated," Annie said.

Every student in the class raised her hand.

"And on the morning of the ballet," Annie went on, "they will dance for Miss Petrovna."

"*Dance?*" Gwen shouted. She and her four friends dropped their hands onto their laps.

"Yes, dance," Annie repeated. "Then Miss Petrovna will personally choose the lucky girl."

"I don't see why we have to dance," McGee grumbled loudly.

"Yeah," Rocky agreed, "especially if all we have to do is walk out three feet and hand her flowers. I mean, how hard is that?"

"This *is* a ballet academy, remember?" Page Tuttle drawled, rolling her eyes at Courtney.

"That's right," Courtney declared. "The flower bearer should be the best dancer in the class. It's only proper."

"No one should be nervous," Annie said. "The steps are very simple. You can learn them in a few minutes."

"How are you going to choose the two girls from this class?" Mary Bubnik asked.

"Well, I thought we should be democratic about it," the pretty ballerina replied. "I'll give you all a few minutes to think about it, then we'll take nominations and vote."

Courtney immediately gathered Page, Alice, and several other girls around her. They pulled together without a backward glance at the rest of the class. Other groups formed near the window.

Mary Bubnik and Zan joined McGee, Rocky, and Gwen in a huddle at the back of the class.

"OK," McGee said in low whisper. "We need to make sure that two of us are picked. So who should we nominate?"

Mary Bubnik raised one finger. "I nominate Zan and Gwen, because Zan knew all about Miss Petrovna's daring escape and Gwen is the oldest."

Zan smiled gratefully but shook her head. "I could never dance in front of Miss Petrovna. I'd be so terribly nervous that I'd lose."

"And you can count me out," Gwen said firmly. "Solo dancing is just not my style." She didn't want to mention that getting up in front of dozens of people in her leotard sounded like the worst possible torture she could imagine. It made her stomach ache just thinking about it.

"Well, I think our nominees ought to be Rocky and McGee," Mary Bubnik whispered. "McGee was such a good leader in our mouse dance."

"Thanks, Mary," McGee said, blushing a bright pink that showed her freckles.

"And Rocky is our best actress," Mary continued.

"Thanks." Rocky punched Mary lightly on the shoulder. She had taken a six-week course in acting at the recreation center on Curtiss-Dobbs Air Force Base. Rocky had learned how to make terrific faces and could even make herself cry when she wanted to. A thoughtful look crossed her face. "I wonder how I should act when I dance for this Petrovna lady?"

"You should definitely act sad," Zan said. "The ballet *Giselle* is a really tragic story. It's about a peasant girl who falls in love with a prince who asks her to be his wife."

"That's tragic?" Gwen asked. "It sounds romantic to me."

"It is, at first," Zan agreed. "Then Giselle finds out that he is already engaged to marry someone else."

"Why, that low-down, two-timin' sneak!" Mary Bubnik drawled, putting her hands on her hips. "So what does this Giselle do?"

"She goes crazy and kills herself."

"Kills herself?" Rocky repeated in disbelief. "I'd kill *him*."

"Me, too!" Gwen agreed.

"Oh, no," Zan said shocked. "She loves him too much. You see, after she dies, she's transported to this strange world filled with the spirits of all the women who have been unhappy in love."

"And *they* kill him?" Rocky asked hopefully.

Zan smiled. "They try to."

"How?" McGee leaned closer to catch all the gory details.

"By making him dance to death."

Mary Bubnik cocked her head. "How could anyone get danced to death?"

"Well, they couldn't very well shoot him," Gwen said sensibly. "The audience paid a lot of money to see him dance."

40

"Besides, it'd be a pretty short ballet, wouldn't it?" McGee said with a grin.

"So how does it end?" Rocky asked.

"Well, Giselle keeps the Prince dancing all night long," Zan explained. "Just when he's about to drop dead, dawn comes and the spirits have to depart. Giselle returns to her grave, and the Prince is left alone, broken-hearted."

"Serves him right," Gwen declared.

Mrs. Bruce struck a resounding chord on the piano to get everyone's attention.

"Are we ready?" Annie asked the class.

The gang nodded and the rest of the girls murmured, "Yes."

"Then let's have the nominations."

Before anyone could open her mouth, Alice Wescott was on her feet, calling out in her loud, nasal voice, "I nominate Courtney Clay — "

"Surprise, surprise," Gwen muttered under her breath.

"And ..." Alice paused for dramatic effect and looked around the room. "Mary Bubnik."

"What?" McGee blurted out, then quickly covered her mouth.

"Me?" Mary Bubnik cried, clapping her hands together with glee. "Y'all really want me?"

Courtney and her friends nodded, with huge grins on their faces. "All right," Annie said, "Courtney Clay and Mary, uh ... Bubnik." She repeated Mary's name slowly to make sure she had it right. Then Annie looked up and asked, "Any more nominations?"

Gwen was about to nominate Rocky and McGee when she saw the look of pure joy on Mary Bubnik's face. She lowered her hand and said nothing.

When no one else spoke up, Annie said, "Well, that makes it easy, then. Our class representatives will be Courtney Clay and Mary Bubnik."

Mary squealed with delight, then turned to her friends. "I knew the Bunheads would come around and start liking us. Oh, you guys, I am *so* happy! I can't wait to tell my mother."

"Courtney and Mary?" Annie called out. "Will you come up here, and I'll fill you in on the details."

Mary skipped up to the front of the room. Rocky turned to the rest of the gang and whispered, "Those Bunheads are up to something."

McGee nodded. "And we'd better find out what it is — *fast.*"

Chapter Five

"I just don't get it," McGee said as she took a place along Hi Lo's counter with Gwen, Zan, and Rocky. Their class was over, but Mary Bubnik had stayed behind to learn her new dance. "I mean, Mary is about the worst dancer in the whole class."

The rest of the girls nodded. The nominations had taken up most of the class hour. Before letting the girls go home, Annie had the class do their exercises at the *barre* and run through a few combinations on the floor.

Zan sighed, "Mary couldn't remember a single one of the steps Annie showed us."

"Even the easy ones," Gwen agreed.

"She kept tripping over her feet," McGee added.

"Those orange knee socks make her mistakes really stand out," Zan said.

McGee giggled. "Like a neon sign."

Suddenly Rocky sat bolt upright on her stool. "Of course!" she declared with a snap of her fingers. "That's it!"

"What?" McGee demanded.

"The only reason the Bunheads nominated Mary," Rocky explained, "was because she is such an awful dancer."

"You mean, they know she'll lose?" Zan asked.

Rocky nodded.

"And that means Courtney is a surefire winner," Gwen finished.

"Right."

"Those jerks!" McGee banged her fist on the counter. "They deliberately want to make a fool of Mary."

"And us," Rocky added. "Because we're her friends."

Zan nodded. "That would be Courtney's own special way of getting us to drop out of class."

"We can't let this happen," McGee said.

"How do we stop it?" Rocky demanded. "Tell Mary Bubnik that they only picked her because she's a lousy ballerina?"

"That would really hurt her feelings," Zan said, shaking her head. "We could never do that."

The four of them slumped over the counter on their elbows. At that moment Mr. Lo came out of the kitchen in the back of the restaurant.

"Greetings and salutations!" he called out.

"Hi, Hi," Gwen greeted him. Saying, "Hi, Hi!" usually made everyone giggle, but right then they were all too depressed to even muster a smile.

"Why so glum, my friends?" he asked, a concerned frown on his face. "Was it a bad first day in class?"

They all nodded.

"Will four of my special Hi Lo hot chocolates, with marshmallows and extra whipped cream, cheer you up?"

Rocky, Zan, and McGee shook their heads. Gwen raised one hand. "Now, wait a minute, they might. Maybe we should try them."

Mr. Lo smiled and hurried back into the kitchen for the milk. They heard his voice call through the pick-up window, "Say, where is my other little friend, Mary Bubnik?"

"She had to stay after class for a special rehearsal," McGee explained.

"I see," Mr. Lo shouted. They heard a clang of a pan against the sink and then his voice, asking, "Is this special rehearsal for something important?"

The four friends exchanged worried looks. "It's very important," Zan whispered.

"You know," Gwen said, "I understand Courtney's nominating Mary, but what about the other classes?"

"That's true," McGee nodded. "She can't control their choices."

"Don't be so sure about that," Zan warned. "Courtney is terribly clever."

"Then we'll just have to keep an eye on her," Rocky said.

A horn honked loudly in front of the shop and everyone jumped.

"Gwen, I think your mom's here," McGee said, peering out the window. "Maybe we'd better cancel our orders."

"My mom?" Gwen looked up at the clock and then called loudly toward the kitchen, "Hi, could I also get a pizza with everything on it, and some chow mein with some fried rice, and a tossed salad?"

Mr. Lo popped his head through the little opening in the wall. "All for you?"

"Yes." Gwen turned to the others, who were staring at her in amazement. "I'm hungry."

Mr. Lo shrugged. "OK, if that's what you want."

"It is." Gwen glanced nervously out the window at her mother. Mrs. Hays was just getting out of the big white Cadillac and making her way carefully across the snowy sidewalk to the door. "One more thing, Hi."

"Yes?"

"Take your time."

The little brass bell tinkled as Mrs. Hays stuck her head in the door. "Gwennie, honey, didn't you hear me honk?"

"Oh, hi, Mom." Gwen acted completely surprised. "Are you here, already?"

"Well, yes." Mrs. Hays pushed up the sleeve of her fur coat and peered at her slim gold watch. "I said I would be back at three-thirty exactly. Put on your coat, Gwendolyn, and let's get going."

"Oh, gee, Mom, I didn't realize it was so late," Gwen said in an overly apologetic voice. "I ordered lunch."

"Lunch? But I thought we were going shopping." Mrs. Hays took out a compact and checked her makeup in a little mirror. "What did you order?"

"A pizza, hot chocolate, chow mein, and a dinner salad."

"What?" Gwen's mother snapped the compact shut. "That's ridiculous. You can't eat that much."

"Watch me."

"Gwendolyn Hays, you cancel that order this minute! And put on your coat!" Mrs. Hays's voice was becoming dangerously shrill. The rest of the girls knew she was really getting angry. They stared at the counter, trying to act like they weren't there.

"I can't cancel, Mother," Gwen insisted. "Mr. Lo's already started cooking everything."

"Now you listen to me, young lady." Mrs. Hays stepped inside the shop and put her hands firmly on her hips. "You and I are going shopping for a brassiere, whether you like it or not."

Brassiere. The ugliest, most embarrassing word in the entire English language and Gwen's mother had just said it out loud. No, Gwen thought to herself, she didn't just *say* brassiere, she *shouted* it.

"Mother, how could you?" Gwen moaned, squeezing her eyes shut.

"What did I say?" Mrs. Hays held her arms out to McGee, Zan, and Rocky on their red leather stools. "What? Brassiere?"

"Mother!" Gwen cried out in anguish as the other three cringed automatically at the sound of *that* word.

"What's wrong?" Mrs. Hays demanded, crossing quickly to Gwen's side and shaking her by the arm.

Gwen kept her eyes shut tight, hoping that maybe her mother would just disappear into thin air or be swallowed up in an earthquake. "Mother, please don't keep saying that word," she managed to plead. "Mr. Lo might hear and there are people in the corner."

Mrs. Hays glanced around in surprise, then lowered her voice to an exaggerated whisper that seemed even louder than her regular voice. "I'm sure they all know what a bra is. But if it makes you feel any better, I won't say it anymore."

Gwen opened one eye and squinted up at her mother. "Thank you."

"We'll just have Mr. Lo wrap up what you have ordered, and then we'll go shopping for a — " Mrs. Hays stopped herself, then said very loudly, "A you-know-what!"

Gwen quickly made a list in her head of ways she could get revenge on her mother. Torture was too kind. It would have to be something really awful, like spilling ketchup on the suede seats of her mother's Cadillac. Or calling up her hairdresser and instructing Toni to dye Mrs. Hays's hair shocking-pink.

Better yet, Gwen would call all of her mother's friends and invite them to a fancy dinner party, then not tell her mother about it. She smiled as she imagined her mother opening the front door, dressed in curlers and cold cream, and seeing all of those dressed-up people staring at her.

That would do it, she thought to herself. Public humiliation. Let her see what it feels like.

"Gwendolyn, are you listening to me?"

With a start, Gwen realized that her mother had been talking to her, but she wasn't sure for how long. She glanced over at her friends, who were sipping their hot chocolates and politely not looking in her direction.

"I just don't understand why you are making such a fuss about this," Mrs. Hays declared. "Sooner or later, every girl has to get a — "

49

"Don't say it!" Gwen pleaded. "Please!"

Her mother leaned down and whispered, "Bra." Then she straightened and continued in her normal voice. "You just have to face up to it, Gwen. Now, either you come with me, or you can just go get it yourself."

Rocky coughed loudly. "Excuse me," she said, "but I could help you buy one, Gwen."

"You?" Mrs. Hays looked at her in surprise.

"Sure," Rocky shrugged. "I think they're cool. I buy 'em all the time." Mrs. Hays raised an eyebrow and Rocky added, "With my mom."

Actually, for six months Rocky had been pestering her mother to let her get a bra. This would be the perfect opportunity to pick out her own.

"You know, Mrs. Hays," McGee joined in. "I've got two older sisters, and I always go with them to buy, uh . . . you know — all of that stuff." McGee had really only gone bra shopping with her sisters once. That's when she'd decided she didn't want to have anything to do with wearing a bra, ever.

"And I've read several magazine articles advising young girls on how to buy . . . *those* kind of things," Zan added helpfully. She had been doing research, because she wanted to be prepared for the day when she would have to get one.

Gwen poked at the little white marshmallows in her hot chocolate and tried to ignore everyone.

She knew what getting a bra meant. It meant she

would have to become a whole different person. First she would have to wear a bra. Then she would get taller. Pretty soon she'd be wearing high heels and nylons and having her hair done once a week, just like her mother. She'd never be able to be just a kid again.

"We could go get the, uh . . ." Rocky searched for the right word ". . . *thing* this week and maybe talk to Mary afterward."

"Great." McGee nodded. "I don't have hockey practice on Wednesday. Let's go then."

"Well, Gwendolyn," Mrs. Hays asked, "what about it?"

"What about what?" Gwen looked her mother straight in the eye.

"Either you go with your friends on Wednesday to get the, uh, *thing.* Or you can come with me right now. What will it be?"

Gwen quickly weighed her options in her head. If she went with her friends, they would find out all about her underwear — what size she wore, what brand, everything. Then again, they probably knew that already from changing together in the dressing room at ballet class. But if she went with her mother, Mrs. Hays would probably announce to the entire store that her daughter was getting her first bra. Just thinking about that made Gwen shudder.

"Well, Gwendolyn?" Her mother tapped her fingers on the counter impatiently.

"I'll go with them on Wednesday." Gwen's voice was barely audible. She figured she had four days to get up her courage to talk about it without dying of embarrassment.

"Mr. Lo?" Mrs. Hays called back into the kitchen. "Is it too late to cancel Gwen's order?"

"It's never too late," Mr. Lo said, sticking his head through the window. "Consider it done."

"Thank you," Mrs. Hays said, pulling her wallet out of her purse. "Let me pay for the girls' hot chocolates, and we'll head home." The girls set their mugs down and went to put on their coats.

"So it's settled then," Zan said, slipping one arm into her coat. "I'll call Mary Bubnik and on Wednesday we can all meet at Baumgartners. They've got the best *things* I know of."

"Some *things* are better left alone," McGee giggled.

Rocky picked up on the joke and grinned. "I'd better look in my closet to see if I've got a *thing* to wear."

"*Things* are looking up!" McGee and Zan said at the same time. The three girls skipped out into the cold afternoon air, giggling the entire way.

Gwen watched them and groaned, "Something tells me this shopping trip is going to be the worst *thing* that ever happened to me."

Chapter Six

On Wednesday, the girls stood huddled together outside the front entrance to Baumgartners, the biggest department store in Deerfield.

"I'm sure glad y'all called me," Mary Bubnik said, her teeth chattering from the cold. "I wouldn't miss this for the world."

"We may have to miss it," Rocky grumbled, checking her watch for the fifth time in as many minutes. "If Gwen doesn't get here soon, we may freeze to death."

"I wonder if she chickened out," McGee said, rubbing her mittened hands together. "I mean, Gwen wasn't too keen on this whole shopping trip."

"She'd better show up," Zan replied. "I spent a

whole week doing research on this." She held several magazines in the air, each filled with slips of paper marking the pages with lingerie advertisements.

Mary Bubnik hopped up and down in place, trying to keep warm. Something unusual across the street caught her eye. "You guys, look at that strange person over there."

"Where?" McGee asked, stomping her feet to get the feeling back in them.

Still bouncing up and down, Mary Bubnik pointed her finger at the jewelry store across the street. They stared intently at a short, stubby girl peering out of the doorway. She was wearing an oversized coat with a fur collar, dark glasses, and a plaid wool hunting hat.

"What is she?" Rocky asked. "A bag lady?"

The bizarre person peered out from the doorway and started to step onto the icy street. At the same moment, a man in a trench coat came out of Baumgartners and the figure retreated back into the shadows.

"Do you think she's sick or something?" Zan mused.

As they watched, the figure reached a gloved hand into her oversized handbag and removed an object that caught the light for a second and glimmered in the sun.

"Hey, it's Gwen," McGee gasped.

"How can you tell?" Rocky squinted across the street.

"Do you see what she has in her hand?" McGee asked.

"A Twinkie!" Mary Bubnik exclaimed. "You're right. It's got to be her."

"And that coat's one that Mrs. Hays wore last winter when our mothers took us to a modeling show," McGee said.

"She must think she's in disguise," Rocky giggled.

"Well, she broke the number one rule for disguises," Zan said, remembering a tip from her Tiffany Truenote stories. "A disguise should make you blend into a crowd, not attract one."

Rocky grinned and cupped her hands around her mouth. "Yo! Gwen!"

The startled figure nearly dropped her snack cake in fright. She quickly ducked back into the shadows.

"We know it's you, Gwen," Rocky yelled. "You can come out now."

Gwen stuck her head out from her hiding place, looked both ways, then scurried across the street. When she reached the group, she whispered hoarsely, "Quick, follow me! The coast is clear."

Without looking to see if they were behind her, Gwen threw open the glass double doors and ran inside Baumgartners. She made a sharp right, ducking behind a display of handbags and scarves.

"What's going on?" McGee demanded as she scrambled up beside Gwen. "And why are you wearing your mother's coat?"

"I don't want anyone to recognize me," Gwen hissed. Across the aisle the rest of the gang peered around the row of purses. "Get down!"

The girls dropped to their knees.

"Is someone following you?" Mary Bubnik asked, her voice sounding a little muffled behind the display.

Gwen shook her head and took off her sunglasses. She had her own wire-rimmed glasses beneath them. "I have been trying to cross the street for the last fifteen minutes. But every time I started to go across, a man would appear."

"So?"

"So." Gwen folded her arms stubbornly. "I am not buying" — she mouthed the next word — "un-der-wear — with a man in the store."

Rocky whistled softly. "That's going to be pretty hard to do. I mean, Baumgartners has got eight floors."

"That's right," McGee chimed in. "I'm sure there are a lot of men that work here, not to mention the ones who come here to shop."

"What?" Gwen nearly fell backward into a revolving rack of belts. As soon as she'd recovered her balance, she gasped. "You don't think they let men work in lingerie, do you?"

"No! Most definitely not," Zan declared. "They probably don't even allow them near the area."

Gwen relaxed and leaned back with a heavy sigh. "Well, that's a relief."

"Come on, you guys," Rocky said, glancing at her watch, "we'd better hurry if we want to get anything before the store closes."

"Right," Zan said. "Follow me."

"Okay," Gwen said, slowly getting to her feet. "But don't walk out in the open."

Zan nodded and led the gang in a snaking pattern across the floor of the store.

"How do you know where you are going?" Mary whispered as they passed between the perfume counters and through the sportswear section.

"I read the floor plan as we came in," Zan replied. "Lingerie is on the third floor and the elevators should be right . . . *here.*"

One side of the store was lined with elevators. Zan stepped confidently up to the call buttons and pushed the one marked "Up." In a few moments, a little bell dinged and the doors slid open. They quickly stepped inside.

"Great," Gwen said. "We've got it all to ourselves."

She spoke too soon. The doors pulled open and a tall man in a pin-striped suit joined them. "What floor did you want, young ladies?" the man asked.

"Three," Rocky replied.

"Six!" Gwen shouted.

"Seven."

"Eight."

Everyone spoke at once. The man looked confused for a moment, then shrugged and pushed the buttons for all of the floors they had named. The elevator hummed and Gwen, with a sinking heart, watched the little numbers rise.

On the third floor, the doors opened and racks of nightgowns, lacy robes, and silky slips spread out before them. The man looked at them expectantly but nobody moved. Gwen stood like a statue, staring straight ahead of her.

After what seemed like an eternity, the doors finally closed. The elevator stopped next on the floor which held the menswear, shoes, and sporting goods sections. Once again Gwen would not budge and after a moment the doors slid shut.

The seventh floor showed dozens of couches, lamps, curtains, and other home furnishings. McGee held her breath, hoping that Gwen would finally make a move. At the rate we're going, she thought to herself, we could be riding this elevator for hours.

Suddenly Gwen cried out, "This is it!" and blocked the closing doors with her foot. They sprang open and she leaped out onto the landing.

"Huh?" Mary Bubnik look really confused. "I thought we were here to — " She was cut short by a sharp dig in the ribs from Rocky.

Gwen spun around, her lips pressed into a tight little smile. "This is where we get the *sofas,* remember?"

"Yeah, then we can get the other *things* later." Rocky arched an eyebrow at the rest of the girls. "Get it?"

As they scrambled off the elevator McGee turned and watched the doors shut. The man in the pin-striped suit had a funny look on his face as he disappeared from sight.

Gwen snapped, "I was not about to get out on the underwear floor with a man watching."

"Well, what do we do now?" Rocky asked, looking around her.

"We could wait for another elevator," Zan suggested. "Or we could take the escalators that are at the center of the store."

"Let's take the escalators," Gwen decided. "But act casual."

Zan led them over to the escalators but another problem soon arose. Every time they started to step onto the moving stairs, a man would come by and Gwen would shriek, "Wait!"

This went on for quite a while until finally McGee had had enough. "Listen, either we go now, or we go home." She stepped onto the escalator and led them back down to the third floor. Gwen meekly followed along with the others.

"Well, we're finally here," Rocky said as they

stepped off the escalator. "And it only took us an hour."

"We could have walked to the top of this store and back in that time," McGee grumbled.

Gwen spun to face them, her sunglasses nearly falling off in the process. "Look, I didn't ask you to do this — you insisted. You're free to leave anytime."

"Touchy," Rocky muttered under her breath.

"There they are!" Zan pointed to the area marked Foundation Garments. "Come on!"

Gwen hid behind two mannequins dressed in negligees and hissed, "You go on without me. I'll just wait here for a second."

"Oooh, you guys, look how pretty everything is!" Mary Bubnik skipped over to a display lined with various styles of bras. "They've got every color of the rainbow here."

"Mary!" Gwen stuck her head out from behind the mannequin and begged, "Please, keep your voice down."

Zan stood on tiptoe, looking for a salesperson. She glimpsed a tall, gray-haired lady ringing up a purchase at the cash register across the room.

"There's a clerk," she whispered. "Let's go ask her for help." Zan started to move toward the register when Gwen grabbed the sleeve of her jacket and yanked her back.

"Are you out of your mind?" Gwen hissed. "I'm not asking a perfect stranger for help."

"What do you plan to do?"

"Just grab one of those *things* off the rack and buy it."

"Aren't you even going to try it on?"

"Not on your life!" Gwen wrapped her mother's coat firmly around her.

"Well, then pick one," Rocky said.

Gwen couldn't bring herself to even look at the bras, let alone touch one. "You pick one for me."

Mary Bubnik grabbed a yellow and pink one. "I love this one. It has little butterflies all over it."

"No, this one is lots better," Rocky insisted, holding up a red satin one covered in black lace.

"Hey, look at this," McGee called loudly over her shoulder. "These are called sports bras." She held up a sturdy white bra with straps that met in the back. "Do you think you play hockey better if you wear one of these?"

"We have to be scientific about this," Zan reminded them, flipping open her magazines to the marked pages. "I think Bali bras have the best advertisments." Her eyes widened and she exclaimed. "Look, you can even get them without straps!"

Rocky peered over her shoulder. "You only need those when you dress up," she declared.

"Are you sure?"

"Sure, I'm sure." Rocky pointed to a woman in the magazine wearing a long evening gown. "See?

Hey, Gwen, you're not planning on wearing this anyplace fancy, are you?"

Gwen was too embarrassed to reply. Her friends, who had promised to help her, were running all over the lingerie department, waving bras in the air, talking in loud voices, and making complete fools of themselves.

"Well, I've narrowed my choices down to three," Mary Bubnik drawled. "The one with the butterflies, the pink-and-white striped one, or this beautiful white lace one. I'd personally love to have them all." She held them up like trophies for the others to examine. "What do you think?"

"I like the sports bra best," McGee said. "But, if I had to choose between your three, I think I'd take the striped one. What does your magazine say about it, Zan?"

"I don't see any with stripes in here," Zan replied, hurriedly leafing through the pages. "You know, I really think Gwen should decide."

"Can I help you, ladies?" A short, stocky woman with close-cropped hair stood behind them. She wore a name tag that said, "Mrs. Elaine Myers, Lingerie." Her request sounded more like an order than a question.

Rocky was the first to speak up. "Yes, we're helping our friend shop for a bra."

"And we've narrowed it down to six choices," McGee added.

The girls each held up their personal favorite.

"What size did you need?"

"Size?" Mary Bubnik repeated.

The woman nodded briskly. "Well, of course. These are all different sizes." She looked them up and down and asked, "Which one of you is this for?"

"Gwen," Mary Bubnik replied. "Gwen, what's your — ?"

The two mannequins were still there but Gwen was nowhere to be seen.

"She's gone," McGee announced.

"Now, where would she go?" Mary Bubnik demanded.

"I'll bet she's hiding somewhere." Rocky knelt down on the carpet to see if she could spot Gwen's shoes sticking out from under any of the racks of clothes.

"This is a lingerie department," Mrs. Myers snapped, "not a playground. If you girls want to play dress-up, I suggest you go to your own homes." As she talked, the woman snatched the different bras from their hands and stacked them on a nearby counter.

"Wait a minute," Mary Bubnik protested, reaching for the butterfly bra the woman had taken from her. "We really are here to buy a bra. It's just that our friend is a little shy."

Just then an unmistakable voice could be heard from the direction of the exits. "How was I supposed to know that room's a restricted area? The sign is so tiny, you'd have to have X-ray vision to see it."

The thin, gray-haired lady they had seen earlier was escorting Gwen by the arm toward the escalator. The man in the pin-striped suit had joined them. He was talking into a walkie-talkie that made crackling noises. "We have a possible code seven on three," he barked into the mouthpiece.

"What's he doing?" Mary Bubnik whispered. "Calling the cops?"

Rocky, whose father was an Air Force security policeman, recognized the code and replied, "No, that just means he has a disturbance on the third floor."

"He's probably asking another store detective to cover for him," Zan added.

"Store detective?" McGee hissed. "Is that what he is?"

"It sure looks like it," Rocky said.

The four of them watched as the gray-haired lady from nightwear, Mrs. Myers from lingerie, and the store detective ushered Gwen up to the register.

"I can't believe they'd let a man into the lingerie department," Mary Bubnik gasped. "Even if he is a detective."

"Poor Gwen," Zan murmured. "She looks just awful."

Gwen was leaning against the counter with her arms folded tightly across her chest. From the way she was biting her lip, they could tell Gwen was trying hard not to cry.

"We've got to rescue her," Rocky declared.

"Right," Mary Bubnik agreed. She pulled a bra off the nearest rack and marched over to the group by the cash register. "We didn't do anything wrong," she said, "we were just shopping."

"You certainly have an odd way of shopping," the detective said, turning to stare at her. His voice was incredibly deep. "I watched you girls come into the store. The first thing you did was crawl through the purse department."

"That because we didn't want to be seen," Mary Bubnik explained.

"Aha!" The gray-haired lady from nightwear raised one bony finger triumphantly.

"No, you don't get it," McGee cut in. "We didn't want to be seen buying a — " She couldn't think of the right words to use in front of a man.

"Feminine support system," Zan finished for her, using a phrase she'd seen in one of the magazines.

"Feminine support system?" the gray-haired lady repeated.

Gwen, who had been unusually quiet, suddenly screeched, "A bra! OK? My mother wants me to get a *bra!* There! I said it!" She turned, faced the entire floor, and shouted, "Bra! Bra! Bra!"

Then Gwen grabbed the brassiere out of Mary's hand and tossed it on the counter in front of the

65

saleslady. "I'm buying one, see? Just tell me how much it is, and I'll pay you."

Gwen was so upset, her hands were shaking. The rest of the gang and the store employees were too stunned by her outburst to react. Mrs. Myers' face softened. She picked up the white bra Gwen had tossed on the counter and said, "This is a size thirty-eight, honey. Shouldn't you be getting something in a junior?"

"OK! OK! Anything you say!" Gwen was near hysteria. "Give me a junior. I don't care; I just want to get out of here!"

McGee, who was standing by a rack full of junior sizes, grabbed one and tossed it to Mrs. Myers. In the meantime, a small crowd had gathered at the edge of the lingerie department. The gray-haired lady patted Gwen on the arm. "Now, there is no reason to get upset. Just take a few breaths and try to calm down."

Gwen snorted in and out a couple of times, but it didn't seem to help. She still felt furious. Furious at the clerks, at her friends, but mostly at her mother for making her endure this agony.

"Oh, look, Mother," a familiar voice sang out from the crowd, "there are those awful girls I was telling you about. It looks like they're in trouble again."

Her voice sent a chill through the entire gang. Slowly they turned. There, smiling smugly at them from the edge of the lingerie department, was Courtney Clay.

Her mother, Cornelia Clay, stood beside her like a mirror image. They wore the same coat, gloves, shoes, and icy smile. The only thing different was their hair. Mrs. Clay wore hers short and shellacked with hairspray. It sat on her head like a large, shiny black hat.

Rocky whispered, "So that's what Bunheads look like when they grow up."

Gwen handed her money to Mrs. Myers, grabbed the bag, and marched stiffly toward the elevator with the gang right behind her. As they passed, Courtney sang out, "What'd you buy, Gwen?"

Gwen stared straight ahead and didn't answer. She wanted to die. Courtney and most of Baumgartners department store knew she had bought a bra. Soon, all of the Bunheads and the whole world would know.

Chapter Seven

The next Saturday, wisps of snow began to fall just as Rocky and her mother left the air base to drive to the ballet studio. By the time their blue Dodge van had reached downtown, the windshield wipers were straining to push the snow off the glass.

Rocky tapped her fingers on the dashboard impatiently. Her mother leaned forward at the wheel, peering intently at the road.

"Can't we go any faster?" Rocky asked. "At this rate, class'll be over by the time we get there."

Her mother just shook her head. "This is not good, not good at all."

Rocky turned up the radio. A deejay's voice blared through the speaker. "Hey, it's lousy out there.

Traffic is backed up along the interstate, and the highway patrol reports three accidents in the last half hour. So take a tip from us here at WDER. Throw a log on the fire, put your feet up, and spend the afternoon at home with the sounds of the fabulous fifties — "

Mrs. Garcia flicked off the radio and looked at her daughter. "Do you hear that, Rochelle? I don't think it's such a good idea for you to take dance today."

"Aw, Mom," Rocky groaned, "we're almost there."

"Yes, but look at this snow!" Mrs. Garcia leaned over and rubbed a gloved hand in a circle on the window by Rocky. "You won't be able to open your door."

She pulled the van up to the curb of Hillberry Hall. A large bank of sooty snow had been pushed to the side by a snowplow.

"Mom, I really think I should just go to the class," Rocky said. "Besides, it's silly to go to all this trouble, then just turn around and go home."

Rocky didn't want to admit it, but she really looked forward to her Saturday ballet lesson. Not that she liked ballet all that much, but her hours at the academy were part of a world that was all her own. With four older brothers who felt they had a right to supervise every aspect of her life at home, that meant a lot.

"The radio says it's going to get worse," Mrs. Garcia continued. "This van is fine for hauling a family of seven but it's not good in the snow. By the time your class is over, we won't be able to move."

Rocky felt a constriction in her chest. She had to stay for two reasons. One, to find a way of helping Mary Bubnik avoid an awful humiliation at the hands of the Bunheads and, two, to see if Gwen was all right. When they'd left Baumgartners on Wednesday, Gwen had refused to speak to any of them. She had marched right out of the store and onto the first bus that passed by.

"Mom, I've got an idea." Rocky picked up her ballet shoes and tucked them into the back pocket of her black jeans. "Why don't you go home, and I'll take a bus back later?" Her mother looked doubtful and Rocky added, "Those buses drive in the snow all the time. They've got those big snow tires, and chains — I'll get home safe and sound."

Mrs. Garcia pushed back a strand of her dark curly hair and smiled wearily at her daughter. After raising four boys, she had long since stopped panicking every time one of her children went off on their own. "OK. But after class, come right home."

"I will." Rocky shoved open the door of the van, and it clunked against the snow bank.

"Now, Rochelle, remember," Mrs. Garcia warned. "I want to see you in the house before dark — and that's an order!"

"Yes, ma'am." Rocky grinned as she squeezed

70

out of the car. Sometimes Mrs. Garcia sounded more like a sergeant than her father.

The wind was blowing briskly as Rocky made her way up the steps. She had to squint to keep the thick falling flakes from blurring her vision. As she walked, Rocky could feel the tip of her nose and her fingers go numb. She wrapped her long scarf even tighter around her neck and hurried up to the entrance.

By the time Rocky reached the third floor of the building and the reception area of the Deerfield Academy of Dance, the feeling had returned to her fingertips. She had hardly stepped inside the office when a hand grabbed ahold of her scarf and dragged her back into the hall.

"Hey, what the — ?"

Zan cut her off. "Sorry about that," she whispered, "I truly meant to catch you before you went inside."

"Did you have to choke me half to death?" Rocky complained, giving the scarf a jerk with her finger to loosen it.

Zan ignored her and said in an urgent voice, "Something really rotten has happened." She hesitated and added, "At least, I think it's happened. I'm not sure."

"What is this, a riddle?"

Zan shook her head vigorously. "It's Courtney Clay, and I'm sure she's up to no good."

"OK, fill me in." Rocky was glad she'd talked her mother into letting her come to class. This sounded interesting. "What's the crime?"

Zan looked over her shoulder and whispered, "Blackmail."

"Who's Courtney's victim?"

"A girl named Jessica White. She's a sixth grade dancer from the Wednesday night class. She also takes technique classes on Saturdays."

"So?"

"So, she is really good. I had her in my class last summer. Her class chose her to be their only representative in the competition."

"The Wednesday class only chose one girl?"

Zan nodded. "Because she is so good, they thought she'd win for sure."

Rocky shrugged. "Well, I guess I'm just glad it won't be Courtney."

"But that's my point." Zan grabbed Rocky's elbow this time and pulled her farther down the hall. "I just heard Jessica tell Miss Delacorte to withdraw her name from the competition. She sounded like she was about to cry."

Rocky twisted one strand of her long, curly hair as she absorbed this information. "Maybe something came up, like a funeral or something."

Zan shook her head impatiently. "I don't think so. I think Courtney did something to make her change her mind."

Rocky cocked her eyebrow. "You sure?"

"Positive."

Rocky looked Zan in the eye for a long moment, then turned and walked back to the door of the Academy. "Come on."

"What are you going to do?"

"Talk to Jessica."

They found her in Studio B, warming up at the *barre*. One of her long legs was stretched out along the top rail and she *pliéd* and *releveéd* onto point with the other. They watched in silence as Jessica turned gracefully to face her outstretched leg, then bent over, placing her forehead on her knee.

Rocky whistled softly in appreciation. "I can see why her class thought she'd win," Rocky murmured out of the corner of her mouth.

"Um . . . excuse me, Jessica?" Zan stepped up to the slender brunette, who stopped her warm-up and looked at the two strangers.

"I'm Suzannah Reed," Zan explained. "We were in class together last summer, remember?"

The girl blinked for a second, then said, "Yes, I remember. You dropped out before the session ended, didn't you?"

"Yes, I had to go on a trip with my parents," Zan said quickly, wincing inside at her little white lie. She had indeed gone on vacation with her family, but the trip had happened later in the summer. The real reason she had dropped out was because Courtney

73

Clay and her friends had started making fun of her in class and in the dressing room. They had teased her so much about her height and gawkiness that finally Zan just couldn't take it anymore and withdrew.

"Too bad you had to leave," Jessica said. "Mr. Anton taught the last two classes, and they were terrific."

"Jessica, this is my friend, Rocky," Zan said, changing the subject. "We want to ask you a question about the competition."

The smile on Jessica's face disappeared. "What about it?"

"I heard you withdraw your name today. Why?"

Jessica stiffened and quickly turned back toward the *barre*. She began doing her *pliés* and *relevées,* staring straight ahead without saying a word.

"You're one of the best young dancers in the school," Zan persisted. "I'm sure you could probably get chosen."

Rocky whispered, "It wouldn't have anything to do with Courtney Clay, would it?"

Jessica jerked her head around and stared at them. Her eyes were wide with fear. "Did Courtney tell you to talk to me?"

"No, we're just trying to find out what she's up to," Rocky replied.

"We're on your side," Zan added encouragingly. "Did she force you to drop out?"

Jessica lifted her leg off the *barre* and slumped back against the wall. The corners of her eyes began to fill with tears. "It's just not fair," she said in a choked voice. "I want to be a member of the Deerfield Ballet more than anything in the world." She looked up at Rocky and Zan. "I've worked really hard for the chance."

"Did Courtney say you wouldn't be chosen?" Zan's eyes grew wide with horror.

Jessica laughed bitterly. "First she asked whether I'd heard anything from the Company's selection committee. Then she said that her mother is a very powerful member of the board of directors for the Deerfield Ballet, and if she wants someone to be in the company — they'll be in the company. She also told me, 'If Mummy decided she didn't like you, well, I guess you'd just have to dance somewhere else.'"

"What's that suppose to mean?" Rocky demanded.

"It means that I have to make sure Mrs. Clay likes me."

Zan cut in. "Like dropping out of the competition so Courtney can be chosen to present the flowers to Alexandra Petrovna."

"Exactly."

Rocky clenched her jaw. "That — that rat!"

"Rat is too nice a word for her," Jessica exclaimed. "I will never forgive her. You know, I thought she was my friend. Courtney doesn't even know the meaning of the word."

Jessica returned to her warm-ups, doing *grand battements,* kicking her legs out fiercely into the air. Rocky and Zan could both imagine who she was pretending to kick.

The girls retreated into the lobby. "We can't let Courtney get away with this," Rocky grumbled. "We should do something."

"But what?"

Zan held out her hands helplessly. "So far the only proof we have that she's trying to rig this audition is that she's hinted things to Jessica and nominated Mary Bubnik."

"Did someone call my name?" The curly-headed blonde stuck her head through the door, her usual grin lighting up her face. Her hair was frosted with snow and flakes still clung to her eyelashes. "Boy, oh, boy, have we got some kind of snowstorm brewing out there!"

"Yeah," Rocky said, looking around the deserted reception area. "We may be the only three who made it to class today."

"Never fear!" McGee leaped into the office and tossed a handful of snow at Rocky. "We are here!" Then she whispered, "Gwen is right behind me. I think she's still a little sore about the you-know-what."

Gwen stepped through the office door and glared at the group.

"A little," Mary Bubnik whispered. "She looks downright mad."

"I just want you to know that I planned to never speak to any of you again," Gwen said, folding her arms across her chest.

"What made you change your mind?" Rocky asked.

"My mother. I decided all of this was her fault, so I'm never speaking to her instead."

"Well, that's a relief," Mary Bubnik said.

"However ..." Gwen held up one hand. "If anybody ever suggests a shopping trip again, you can count me out."

"It's a deal." Rocky gave Gwen a thumbs-up sign.

At that moment, Miss Delacorte, the Russian receptionist, rushed into the office. She had her familiar chiffon scarf wrapped around her head.

"My goodness, but it is freezing out there. Brrrr!" Miss Delacorte hugged her arms around her shoulders and then looked hard at the girls. "What are you all do-ink out here? Class should have begun already."

Zan spoke up. "The studio seems practically deserted. I guess a lot of people decided to stay home because of the snow."

"They were smart," Miss Delacorte said, untying

77

her scarf. "We all must be cuckoo to come out in this blizzard."

"Blizzard?" Zan repeated.

"Certainly. Haven't you looked outside? It's snowing cats and dogs."

McGee giggled. "I think you mean *raining* cats and dogs."

"No, I mean, snowing," Miss Delacorte repeated. "Big, white flakes." She hung her heavy wool coat on the rack by the door and said, "You girls should leave your coats out here to let them dry and go change your clothes."

All of the girls removed their jackets except Gwen. She kept hers zipped up tight with her arms folded in front of her.

"Aren't you going to take off your coat?" McGee asked, as they made their way to the dressing room.

Gwen shoved her glasses up on her nose. "I'd rather not."

"Why?" Mary Bubnik asked.

"My mother made me wear my new bra," Gwen mumbled. "I don't want the Bunheads to know."

"Aw, they'll never even notice," McGee said, patting her on the back. "I didn't."

Gwen's arms were still folded firmly across her chest. "That's because I'm wearing my coat. Anyway, Courtney saw me buy it. I know she'll make fun of me."

"Hey, Gwen, it's no big deal," Rocky said. "People

wear bras all the time. Courtney has probably for-
gotten all about it."

"Are you sure?"

Rocky nodded. "Sure I'm sure."

Gwen gingerly removed her jacket and clutched
it in front of her.

"See?" McGee said. "Nobody will know a thing."

Rocky threw back the curtain to the dressing
room and everyone froze.

The whole room had been decorated with what
looked like white streamers. They were draped
across the mirrors and dressing table and one hung
from the light fixture. They realized, to their horror,
that the streamers weren't crepe paper but white,
cotton . . .

"Bras!" Mary Bubnik gasped. "The Bunheads
have covered this entire room with brassieres!"

Chapter Eight

"That does it!" Rocky said, yanking the last of the white bras off the mirror and tossing it to McGee. "I say we march into class and rearrange Courtney's legs."

"Good idea." McGee stuffed the bra in the trash can by the dressing table. "That way she won't be able to dance in the competition."

"I can't believe someone could be that cruel," Zan said, shaking her head.

"Do y'all think it's possible that Courtney did this as a joke?" Mary Bubnik asked hopefully. "You know, just to kid Gwen?"

"Some joke," Rocky said, practicing a karate kick

in the air. "I bet she's in there right now, just waiting to get the last laugh."

McGee nodded. "They want to see how upset we are."

"Hey!" Zan snapped her fingers. "Why don't we disappoint them? You know, pretend that we never saw their decorations."

"You mean, act like we just arrived?" Mary Bubnik asked.

"Good thinking!" McGee grabbed her coat and put it on over her leotard and tights. "Then when they're least expecting it — "

"We punch their lights out!" Rocky chopped in the air. "I like that idea."

"I think punching their lights out is a little harsh," Mary Bubnik said as she slipped her arms into her own faded jacket.

Rocky zipped up her red satin jacket and wrapped her scarf around her neck. "I don't. They deserve it."

"What do you think, Gwen?" McGee asked.

Gwen, who had been slumped on the wooden bench by the door ever since they'd entered the dressing room, blinked at them from behind her glasses. "I think — " she paused and tilted her head — "I think I'd like to go home now for about twenty years."

"Why?" Mary Bubnik asked.

Gwen's voice was soft and her eyes had a faraway look in them. "After twenty years, I'll be all grown up, out of school, and all of this will be just a stupid memory."

Rocky punched Gwen on the shoulder. "Stop talking like that, OK?"

"Geez Louise!" McGee pulled her to her feet. "You can't give up now."

Mary Bubnik nodded. "You've got to go into the classroom."

"Otherwise those Bunheads will have won." Rocky slammed her fist into her hand. "And that would be awful."

Gwen, who still had her arms crossed firmly over her chest, said, "OK, I'll go in there. But I'm not taking off my coat."

"All right." McGee shrugged. "But you might get hot."

"I don't care!" Little beads of perspiration were already forming on Gwen's forehead. Underneath her parka she had layered a T-shirt, a sweatshirt, and a heavy cotton sweater in an effort to hide the horrible bra. That morning her brother had called her "Pillsbury Doughboy," but Gwen didn't care. She wasn't about to let the Bunheads get another laugh at her expense.

"Now, the truly important thing," Zan said as she put her lavender beret back on her head, "is to act like nothing has happened. We'll say we're late because our car got stuck in the snow. They'll believe that."

"And we had to run all the way." McGee started jogging vigorously. "It might help if we seem a little out of breath."

Gwen halfheartedly trotted in place while the rest of the girls ran in frantic circles around the room.

"Pinch your cheeks, everybody," Mary Bubnik instructed, "so it looks like you've been out in the cold."

As they jogged together to the studio, Zan said, "The most difficult thing we have to do is act happy to see the Bunheads."

"Never!" Gwen's knees locked.

"I know it's hard," Rocky said. "But you want to get back at the Bunheads, don't you?"

Gwen nodded vehemently.

"Then smile!"

Gwen forced her lips into a fiendish grin. The others did the same. Then all five of them raced into the studio.

"Sorry we're late, Annie!" McGee huffed. "But our car got stuck."

Rocky fell against the ballet *barre* dramatically. "I can hardly breathe, we ran so fast."

Zan bent over, pretending to catch her breath. "We changed our clothes in the car — "

" — and came straight into the studio." Mary Bubnik waved one hand in front of her face, acting overheated.

Gwen's face was frozen in a smile, and she just stood there grinning at the Bunheads.

"That's fine," Annie said. "I'm just glad you could join us. As you can see, only a few other brave souls made it today." Mrs. Bruce, the pianist, and most of the rest of their class hadn't shown up.

Courtney, Alice, and Page were standing by the *barre* and disappointment was clearly written across their faces. The Bunheads huddled together for a conference.

"You girls just take a few minutes to catch your breath and take off your coats and then we'll begin." Annie knelt by a little record player at the front of the classroom.

All of the gang removed their coats and piled them on the piano bench, except Gwen. She took her place at the *barre* in her overstuffed jacket.

As Annie blew some dust off the needle of the record player, Courtney suddenly sang out, "Annie, does it seem cold in here?"

"Not really," their teacher answered without looking up. "Why?"

"Well, I was just wondering," Courtney said, turning to face Gwen with a smug smile. "Why won't Gwen take off her coat?"

"I'd rather not," Gwen explained quickly. "I'm cold."

"Oh, really?" Courtney arched her eyebrows and Page and Alice burst into giggles. Gwen's ears turned bright pink.

"Are you all right, Gwen?" Annie asked.

"I'm fine," Gwen snapped, her face growing redder and redder. "Can't a person have a little chill without everyone making a big deal out of it?"

"I think it's freezing in here," McGee announced suddenly. She turned to Zan and Rocky and asked meaningfully, "Don't you?"

"Brrr!" Rocky nodded. "Look, I can almost see my breath in here." She puffed her cheeks noisily and blew into the air.

"You know, my legs are numb," Zan added. "I should have brought my leg warmers."

"Gee," Mary Bubnik said, "I don't think it's that cold — "

"Oh, yes, you do!" Rocky looked Mary right in the eye.

"I — I do?" Mary stammered.

"You do!" Rocky repeated, tossing a look over at Gwen.

"Oh." Mary's eyes widened and she repeated, "*Oh!* You know, you're right. It *is* cold in here." She jumped up and ran for the coats. "I'm going to put on my jacket before I catch cold."

"What a bunch of liars," Page Tuttle murmured to Courtney.

"Who are you calling liars?" Rocky demanded in a low, tense voice. Her hands were clenched at her sides.

Zan ran to the window and shouted, "For your information, there is a blizzard out there, and we could all freeze to death."

At the end of her sentence she turned to gesture dramatically toward the window and stopped. "Wow!" she gasped. "There truly *is* a blizzard out there."

The rest of the girls all ran to the window to look. The snow was swirling so fast and hard that they could barely see the street three floors below.

"I've never seen it snow this hard," Courtney murmured.

"Now, there's no need to be concerned," Annie announced. "It looks much worse from up here." She draped her arms around Mary Bubnik and Gwen and said, "You know, this gives me an idea."

Their teacher ran back to the record player and, after thumbing through the records, put one of them on the turntable. As the music began to play she said, "In dance, we tell wonderful stories, not with words, but with our bodies. Let's tell the story of what is happening outside today."

They watched her skip and whirl around the room as a flute filled the air with delicate notes of music.

"I get it," Rocky whispered. "She's playing like she's a snowflake."

Courtney and Page joined Annie, fluttering their arms like fragile little crystals of snow. Alice hesitated for a moment, then tiptoed across the floor, making little leaps from time to time.

The gang just stood there without making a move. Rocky and McGee didn't want to embarrass themselves. In her padded suit, Gwen didn't feel much like dancing. Zan's fear of performing gripped her whole body and she stood frozen. Mary Bubnik couldn't think of a single dance step. Her mind was a complete blank. The moment she thought of a movement, one of the Bunheads would do it, and she didn't want to look like a copycat.

"It's not so hard," Annie called encouragingly. "Don't think so much. Let your body think for you."

The girls continue to stand stiffly in a little group. Annie smiled and suggested, "Try this idea. What does winter remind you of?"

A little light went on in McGee's eyes. With a grin she stepped onto the dance floor and pretended to skate as if she were moving a hockey puck toward an imaginary goal. She made a sweeping slap shot, then raised her hands in triumph over her head.

"Goal!" Annie cried out, clapping her hands together. "Very good, McGee."

87

Rocky leaped out onto the floor and hopped from side to side like a skier. "Hey, this is kind of fun," she yelled.

Courtney, not to be outdone, dropped to the floor and began to wave her arms up and down.

Page Tuttle cried, "Snow angels!"

Mary Bubnik rolled a tiny ball of snow until it became huge. As she started rolling another one, Zan joined in. Together they sat that ball on top of the imaginary large one. Meanwhile Gwen and Rocky made a small one and placed it on top. McGee mimed placing a hat, eyes, and carrot nose on the imaginary creature.

"It's Frosty the Snowman," Annie cried with delight.

Alice Wescott fluttered by and said, just loud enough for the girls to hear, "Funny, it looks just like Gwen."

"But it's missing something," Courtney said, dancing around the pretend snowman.

"What's that?" Mary Bubnik demanded.

Courtney whispered something to Page, who broke out into a wide grin. Then Courtney grabbed something out of the air and pretended to slip it on the snowman. First she mimed putting straps over the arms and then hooking it in the back.

"That looks like a bra!" Mary said out loud.

Page and Courtney howled with laughter and danced off to the other side of the room.

Gwen forced herself to smile, but her chin started to quiver and she felt an awful tenseness in the back of her throat.

"*Don't cry!*" she repeated over and over to herself, all the while smiling at Courtney.

"That does it," Rocky declared. "They can't treat Gwen like that."

"What are you going to do?" Mary Bubnik asked.

"We tried being nice and ignoring their little jokes," McGee said. "It didn't work."

"Now it's *war!*" Rocky bent over and scooped up an imaginary handful of snow. She carefully packed it into a snowball, then called, "Hey, Courtney!"

As Courtney spun to face her, Rocky threw the imaginary snowball with all her might.

Courtney saw the look on Rocky's face and instinctively ducked. This made the gang hoot with laughter.

Within seconds the class had erupted into a full-fledged snowball fight, with the girls ducking and hurling imaginary balls at each other.

"I got you!" McGee shrieked as she pelted Page with five balls in a row.

"Did not!" Page put her hands on her hips and shouted back.

"Did so!"

The two teams had completely stopped dancing and were shouting at each other over the music.

"Liar!"

"No, you're the liar!"

"Girls!" Annie clapped her hands together to restore order. "Girls, please."

At the same time, Miss Delacorte stuck her head through the door and shouted, "Well, dar-links, it is official. We are snowed in!"

They all turned to stare at her.

"The phone has not stopped ring-ink. All of your parents are calling to say wait here, they will come for you as soon as they can get through." From behind her came the sound of the phone, and she threw her hands in the air. "Oh! There it goes again. Remember, you are to stay put!"

The girls moved to the window to watch the gray sky swirl outside. The sidewalks below were completely deserted. A lone car, its headlights sending feeble shafts of light into the snowfilled air, crept slowly along the street.

"I read a book once called *Snowbound*," Zan said quietly. "That's what this feels like. We could be here for days."

"Or weeks," McGee added.

"Or even months!" Mary Bubnik drawled.

"With you?"

The two groups pointed at each other.

"Oh, no!"

Chapter Nine

"It's a good thing I packed a full supply of snacks," Gwen declared as she dug into her blue canvas dance bag. "You never know when you're going to get stranded like this."

As she spoke she laid her supplies out in front of her—two packages of Twinkies, three Snickers bars, a bag of M&Ms and a large plastic bag of trail mix.

"You could survive a whole week on that," McGee marveled, reaching into the trail mix.

"My motto is, 'Be prepared!' " Gwen passed her food around the circle. Courtney and the Bunheads eyed the treats with envy.

Gwen, who still smarted from their teasing, turned to Courtney and said in her sweetest voice, "Gee,

Courtney, I'd really like to offer you some of this — "

"But Gwen knows how concerned you are about your weight," Rocky added with glee. She took a big bite of a candy car and mumbled, "You being a ballerina and all."

Courtney's face revealed her disappointment for only a moment. Then she folded her arms across her chest and sniffed, "That's true. I never eat junk food because it's so bad for you."

"Suit yourself." Gwen shrugged and popped a handful of the M&Ms in her mouth. "But we could be here for hours, and I doubt if Herb's Health Food Restaurant is making deliveries in this weather."

Alice and Page hungrily watched the gang enjoy their treats. Finally Alice scooted away from Courtney and said, "I don't have a weight problem. I can eat anything!" She stuck her hand into the bag of M&Ms. "Thanks, Gwen, I really appreciate this."

"I never said I had a weight problem," Courtney snapped. "I just said I don't eat all that unhealthy sugary stuff."

"Well, if we're going to be here for hours" — Page Tuttle stood up and stretched her arms casually as she edged closer to the gang and the food — "I guess it wouldn't hurt to have a little something to eat." She glanced at Courtney and added, "For energy."

Page helped herself to some of Gwen's trail mix

and soon the whole room was munching happily on the different treats.

Courtney sat in the corner scowling. Not only had her own friends deserted her, but now she was the only one left out of the impromptu picnic on the dance floor.

Annie remembered that a jar of orange juice was still in the staff refrigerator. She quickly ran and got it, then poured them all a drink in little paper cups. "This reminds me of slumber parties," she said with a giggle. "You know, where we'd stay up all night and tell each other scary stories."

"Ooh, does anyone know any?" Mary Bubnik asked.

"I know one," Zan replied, taking a sip of her orange juice.

"Tell us," McGee urged. The circle tightened as the girls moved closer.

"Once there was a man who had a truly faithful dog named Rex," Zan began.

"That *is* terrifying." Courtney rolled her eyes at Page. "I'm shaking in my shoes."

Zan ignored her and went on. "The man lived on a cliff by a swift river. One night he slipped and fell in. He didn't know how to swim and cried for help, but no one came. Then his dog Rex leaped in and pulled him over to the bank. The man was saved, but his dog was dragged under by the current and never seen again."

"Oh, that's sad," Mary Bubnik said with a slight sniffle.

"The man was truly heartbroken. He vowed never to forget his faithful dog, so he built a statue of Rex on his front lawn. Lots of years passed. The man got married and his wife had a baby. Soon he forgot all about his faithful dog Rex."

She lowered her voice to a dramatic whisper and the others strained to hear. "Then one dark night a kidnapper broke into their house. He tied up the man and his wife and, snatching up their baby, ran out the front door. But something incredible happened. They could hear the sounds of a terrible fight going on outside, horrible screaming and shouting, and the cries of their little girl."

"Oh, that's awful," Gwen said. "They couldn't do anything to stop it because they were all tied up."

"Right," Zan agreed. "They were sure that the kidnapper was hurting their baby. Finally they got loose and ran out after him. They found the bad man dead on the lawn, his clothes all ripped to pieces."

"What happened to the baby?" McGee demanded anxiously.

"The baby was fast asleep at the foot of the statue of the dog. But here is the strange part. Between the marble jaws of the statue was a piece of material torn from the clothes of the kidnapper."

Gwen shivered. "You mean, the ghost of his dog saved their baby?"

Zan nodded. "Rex remained ever faithful, ever loyal — even after death."

"Geez Louise!" McGee whistled softly under her breath. "That's kind of scary, and neat, all at the same time."

"Oh, really?" Courtney said. "Sounds like a rerun from *Lassie* to me."

Mary Bubnik shook her head. "I don't think our dog Pete would ever do anything like that. He's scared of his own shadow."

"I liked the story," Rocky declared.

"I thought it was boring," Courtney said with a yawn. She turned to Page and said loudly, "Wake me when we get to something interesting."

"I have a true story," a voice said from the edge of the circle. The whole group jumped.

"Miss Delacorte," Annie said. "We didn't hear you come in. Join us."

Miss Delacorte pulled a chair into the circle and sat with her hands folded in her lap. The gray afternoon light cast dramatic shadows over her pale, lined face.

"My story begins in Russia."

Zan felt a little tingle go up her spine. She loved stories about foreign countries.

"The year was nineteen-twenty." The older lady put one hand to her face. "Oh, so very long ago! The Ballet Russe was the toast of Europe. Many young men came from around the world to join the dance company. One of them was Ivan Scapinsky. And *that* is who this story is about."

Miss Delacorte paused to take a breath, and the girls shifted position. Gwen took a bite of her Twinkie and passed the cake to the rest of the gang. They chewed quietly, listening to Miss Delacorte's story.

"Ivan Scapinsky grew up in a small village in Russia. Ever since he was little he wanted to be a dancer. His one goal in life was to dance with the Ballet Russe. So he said good-bye to his native country and off he went to Paris."

The wind whistled between the panes of glass in the windows.

"Ivan was very lucky. The Ballet Russe welcomed him with open arms and took him on their tour of America."

Miss Delacorte clasped her hands to her throat, a wonderful smile lighting up her face.

"Just think of it! A young man dreams of joining the greatest ballet in the world, of dancing wonderful parts, of seeing the world — and all his dreams come true! Oh, yes, Ivan was very lucky." Her voice dropped to a whisper. "Until that fateful night. . . ."

The girls in the room held their breath and waited for Miss Delacorte to go on.

"It happened during a rehearsal in the dead of winter. There was a terrible storm as they loaded their scenery into the theatre. Oh, it was the worst of conditions. The dancers were cold and sick, but they had a performance that night and they needed to practice."

Miss Delacorte sighed heavily. Her eyes had a far-away look in them as if she were traveling back in time.

"Thunder and lighting crashed outside as they began their rehearsal. Young Ivan stepped onto the stage and did his first *tour jeté,* leaping high into the air. And then — it happened."

"He sprained his ankle?" Page whispered.

Miss Delacorte raised her eyebrow and Page shut up.

"Lightning flashed, and the lights went out. There was a terrible silence. Then the fuse box exploded and fire broke out. People were screaming and running everywhere. The scenery started to collapse but Ivan held on to it and kept it standing. He shouted directions to the dancers, guiding them toward the exits, all the while fighting to keep the scenery up. No one knew what gave him the strength to do it. The scenery weighed thousands of pounds. But Ivan knew that if he let go, many people would be hurt. In the end, everyone managed to get out safely — except Ivan."

"What happened?" Rocky asked.

"Did he die?" Gwen whispered.

"No." Miss Delacorte shook her head sadly. "For Ivan, it was much worse. The ropes holding the lighting instruments above his head burned through and they dropped on him, breaking his leg in several places. Ivan Scapinsky lived, but he was never able to dance again."

"That's sad," Zan said.

"But it's not really scary," Courtney observed.

"Ah, but I am not finished." Miss Delacorte raised one finger. "I have not told you the part that affects you."

"Us?" Gwen nearly choked on the last bite of her Twinkie.

"Yes, you. You see, the theatre that burned was here in Deerfield. It stood on this very spot."

The girls all shivered unconsciously.

"Ivan's career was finished, but he never stopped loving the ballet. He stayed here in Deerfield and every dancer in every company that came through town knew of his heroic act. They invited him to watch their ballets from backstage. For fifty years, Ivan never missed a performance."

Miss Delacorte stood up. "Ivan walked with a cane and had to drag his crippled leg behind him. It sounded like this." Miss Delacorte lifted her left leg and dropped it on the floor with a loud *thunk*, then dragged it behind her. "Thunk. Drag."

"Thunk. Drag," Rocky imitated her out loud.

Miss Delacorte nodded. "That's right, just like that." She sat on the edge of the chair and leaned forward. "Ivan died nearly ten years ago.

But here is the strange part." She dropped her voice to a whisper. "He still never misses a performance."

"What do you mean?" Courtney asked in a shaky voice.

"In the theatre, when the orchestra begins the overture, the dancers can hear him taking his familiar place backstage. It is a much quieter sound now, but it is Ivan."

Mary Bubnik let out a little squeal and clutched Zan's arm.

Miss Delacorte looked down at her hands and continued. "Sometimes, when I am working late here in the studio, I am sure that Ivan is with me." She closed her eyes and murmured, "I listen close and can almost hear him breathing."

McGee could feel the little hairs on the back of her neck stand up. Mary Bubnik and Gwen sat frozen, and Zan's eyes were two big circles.

Miss Delacorte looked like she was in a trance. "At times like those I whisper, 'Ivan, is that you?' " She cupped her hand around her mouth and called softly, "Ivan! Speak to me!"

"Stop it, please," Alice Wescott whined. "You're scaring — !"

Alice's last word was drowned out by a fierce gust of wind that rattled the windows. The building shuddered and the girls all screamed. And then the lights went out.

Chapter Ten

"Girls, please!" Annie called over their cries. "Screaming isn't going to turn the lights back on."

"It looks like it's just our building," Miss Delacorte declared in the darkness. The elderly woman stood silhouetted in the window, and the fading light outside gave her a ghostly appearance.

"Maybe it's just a fuse," Annie suggested.

"I'll go to the office and call the custodian," Miss Delacorte said.

"Good idea. I'll check the floors below. The custodian might be down there."

"Annie, don't leave us!" a voice wailed from the darkness. "I'm afraid of the dark."

Zan recognized the voice. She whispered to Gwen, "That's Courtney!"

"I can't believe it," Gwen whispered back. Gwen felt across the floor and tapped McGee on the knee to pass the news.

Meanwhile Zan told Mary Bubnik. Their whispering was covered by the sound of Courtney whimpering, "Someone, *please* turn on the lights!"

"Now, girls, stay calm." Annie Springer's voice came from the vicinity of the door. "Miss Delacorte and I are going to find out what's wrong. We'll be back in just a minute. I want you all to stay put. Don't try to move around. You could get hurt."

The floor creaked as the two ladies left the studio. Then the room fell deathly quiet. All the girls sat still, peering out into the darkness.

Mary Bubnik was straining so hard to see that little gray dots swirled in front of her eyes. She scooted closer to Zan on the floor and tried to ignore the loud thumping of her heart.

There was a loud crash from the reception area.

"My goodness, that hurt!" a voice complained. It was Miss Delacorte. Odd little slapping sounds followed.

In her mind's eye Zan could see the receptionist feeling her way through the dark with her hands.

Then there came the sound of a drawer being opened and the rustle of papers and little boxes being pushed around.

"Now, where could that flashlight be? Think, you silly goose!"

Zan stifled a giggle. Miss Delacorte was talking to herself in the dark. There was something comforting about the sound of the old lady's voice. Beside her, Zan heard a throaty chuckle that she guessed was Rocky.

Suddenly another sound caught Zan's attention. She cocked her head and listened. The rest of the girls heard it, too. There was a hollow thud, followed by a soft, swishing sound. It sounded like it was in the room with them.

Mary Bubnik grabbed Zan by the left hand and Gwen grabbed her right. They held their breath and waited for the sound to happen again.

It did, only this time it was a little louder.

Thunk. Drag.

"Do you hear that?" Page Tuttle whispered. Gwen, Zan, and Mary Bubnik all nodded in the darkness.

Rocky cocked her head, trying to determine where the sound was coming from.

Thunk. Drag.

The sound was now by the door and moving along the far wall. Rocky crawled toward it as quietly as a cat.

Thunk. Drag.

Now it was moving toward the piano. Rocky veered in a diagonal to head it off.

"Ivan Scapinsky?" Page called shakily. "Is that you?"

She was answered by the sound of harsh breathing, rasping in and out.

"That's his breathing," Page groaned. "Just like Miss Delacorte said!"

"Go away!" Alice squealed. "We don't want you here!"

"Alice!" Courtney shrieked. "Turn on the lights this instant!"

"I can't," Alice replied with a whimper.

"I'm sure, if that *is* Ivan Scapinsky," Mary Bubnik said loudly, "he doesn't want to hurt us. He *likes* dancers. Miss Delacorte said so."

"But we're not really dancers," Gwen blurted out. "I mean, my mother forced me to take ballet, but I never really liked it." After a moment of hesitation she added, a little more loudly, "Until now. Now I *love* ballet."

"Yes, we love ballet!" Page echoed. "I've taken classes since I was six. That should count for something."

"Stop it, all of you!" Courtney barked.

Rocky crouched in a taut ball, listening. Then like a lightning bolt she shot her hand out and grabbed in the darkness.

"Ouch!"

Rocky held tight to the ankle she'd captured, and felt the foot with her hand. It was wearing a ballet shoe. Then she patted up the leg. At the knee she discovered a huge hole in the leg of the tights. A big grin crept across her face.

"McGee?" she whispered. "I knew it was you!"

Meanwhile the other girls were too wrapped up in their pleas for mercy to hear a thing.

"I am starting my diet tomorrow," Gwen swore solemnly, "I have eaten my last Twinkie."

"Of course, I know I've always been a klutz," Mary Bubnik chattered nervously. "I mean, I can't even do a forward roll, so gymnastics was out and baton twirling and tap were a disaster. But all that's changing, Mr. Scapinsky. My very own class nominated me for the flower bearer competition. It's a big honor and everything. So I must be getting better, just to be considered for it. And — "

"Oh, Mary Bubnik, shut up!" Courtney's voice cut through the air.

Rocky made up her mind then and there to get Courtney. Rocky grabbed McGee by the hand and together they advanced on Courtney.

THUNK. Drag. THUNK. Drag.

"Oh, no, oh, no, oh, no," Alice Wescott repeated to herself, over and over.

Rocky took a deep breath and croaked hoarsely, "Court-ney! *Court*-neeee!"

Mary Bubnik and Gwen were talking so much

they they didn't recognize Rocky's voice. But Zan did. She felt for their faces and covered their mouths with her hands.

"It's OK," Zan whispered, "it's Rocky." She waited until she could feel them relax, then she let go. The three of them sat quietly, waiting to see what would happen next.

THUNK. Drag. THUNK. Drag.

Still holding hands, Rocky and McGee made their way toward the circle.

"He's coming closer!" Alice Wescott squealed.

"Courtney Cla-a-a-y!" Rocky added a ghostly quiver to her voice. "What have you been up to?"

Courtney was silent.

"Ivan's talking to you," Page Tuttle cried. "Courtney, answer him!"

"I — I can't," Courtney whimpered. "Leave me alone."

THUNK. Drag. THUNK. Drag.

"Court-neeeeee!" Rocky wailed. "What about the competition?"

"Wha-wh-what about it?" Courtney stammered in the tiniest voice.

"Courtney, Ivan wants you to answer him," Alice pleaded.

"What have you been doing to the other girls in the competition?" the ghostly voice continued.

"Courtney?" Page clutched at her friend's arm. "What's he talking about?"

"I don't know, I just don't know," Courtney hissed. "I've got to get out of here."

"Don't leave me!" Alice cried, grabbing a hold of Courtney's leotard. Three frightened girls stumbled in an awkward huddle toward the door.

THUNK. Drag. THUNK. Drag.

Rocky and McGee put themselves between the Bunheads and the exit. They weren't about to let them out of the room.

"What did you say to Jessica White?" Rocky persisted.

"Wha — ? Nothing, nothing at all!" Courtney cried.

Page squeezed Courtney's arm. "Tell him," she hissed. "Please, tell him! Maybe he'll go away."

"I didn't mean anything," Courtney whimpered. "I just warned her — "

"The window!" Mary Bubnik suddenly shrieked. "Look!"

All of them saw it at the same time. There, dimly silhouetted against the window, was the figure of a man moving behind the curtain. McGee and Rocky forgot about their act and screamed in terror right along with the others.

Gwen threw her blue canvas tote bag in the ghost's direction, which inspired the Bunheads. They had left their dance bags by the door. Page grabbed hers and Courtney followed suit. Screaming with all their might, they ran toward the window.

"Go away!" Courtney shrieked. She swung her bag into the darkness. "We don't want you here."

"Yeah," Page said, flailing blindly at whatever was near her. "Leave us alone, you creep!"

"Take that!" Alice shouted. "And that and that!"

"Ooof! Ouch!" a man's voice cried out. "Stop that!"

There was a loud humming sound, and the fluorescent lights suddenly flickered back on. The room was filled with light, and the girls blinked at the sudden change.

"We've got him!" Courtney cried, clutching a figure draped in the long black curtains hanging by the window. "Somebody get Annie." Page and Alice struggled to help Courtney keep the man tangled up.

"Let go of me this instant!" the man roared. His feet were visible beneath the black drape. He was wearing ballet shoes and a pair of familiar gray pants.

"Good work, Courtney," McGee sang out happily. "You've captured Mr. Anton."

"Ha. Ha. Very funny," Courtney replied.

"This is no joke," Mr. Anton bellowed from inside the curtain. "Release me — *now!*"

Courtney and Page sprang back in horror. There was a flurry of arms as Mr. Anton beat the curtain away from his body.

"What's the meaning of this?" he demanded of the room at large.

"Ask them," Rocky said, gesturing toward the Bunheads.

"Mr. Anton, I — I had no idea it was you back there," Courtney stammered.

"Well, of course it was me," he snapped impatiently. "I was searching for the fuse box. Who did you think it was?"

"Ivan Scapinsky," Courtney answered in a tiny voice.

"Who?" he demanded.

"The ghost of Ivan ..." Courtney looked to the rest of the room for help.

"Never heard of him," Gwen said with a shrug.

"This is no way to behave in a ballet studio." Mr. Anton rubbed his arm where a red welt had appeared. "Hitting me with your dance bags." He looked directly at Courtney and shook his head. "Really."

Courtney's face turned beet-red.

Mr. Anton announced to the rest of the room, "Some of your parents have arrived to pick you up. I expect you to leave this classroom in an orderly fashion." He stomped out of the studio and seconds later Courtney raced for the dressing room.

"Give me five!" McGee and Rocky slapped hands in the air.

"That was really rotten," Page hissed in their direction.

108

Zan put her hands on her hips. "Serves you right for being so mean to Gwen."

"Yeah," Rocky said. "I think Courtney should know that if you do battle with us — you'll lose." She jabbed the air with a karate kick for emphasis.

"I wouldn't be so sure about that," Page said, crossing her arms.

"Yes," Alice nodded. "Next Saturday is the competition, and Courtney's a shoo-in."

"How can you say that?" Gwen asked. "There will be lots of girls competing."

"That's what you think." Page smiled smugly. "The girls from the Monday and Wednesday classes withdrew their names last week."

"What!" Zan's eyes widened.

"Then who's left?" Rocky asked.

"Courtney Clay," Page said in a sickeningly sweet voice. "And Mary Bubnik."

The gang watched Page and Alice flounce out of the room. Voices came from the reception area as parents started to arrive to take their children home.

"Maybe they're lying," Rocky said hopefully.

"And maybe they're not," Gwen groaned.

"Well," Mary Bubnik giggled, "at least I've got a fifty-fifty chance of winning."

The four girls turned and stared at her open-mouthed.

Chapter Eleven

On Tuesday afternoon, Zan hurried to Hi Lo's. She had called an emergency meeting of her friends, excluding Mary Bubnik, and didn't want to be late. Mrs. Hays dropped Gwen and McGee off in front of the restaurant just as Zan arrived.

"Thanks for coming on such short notice." Zan threw open the glass door, and the brass bell tinkled above her head. The cold January wind blew them all inside.

Mr. Lo peeked out through the kitchen window and called, "Greetings and salutations. Pull up a stool. I'll be right with you."

The front door swung open again. It was Rocky, her wild hair looking as if she'd been caught in a hurricane. "Sorry I'm late, guys. My dumb brother didn't give me the message till after school today."

"Your arrival was perfectly timed," Zan said, removing her lavender beret and gloves. "We just got here ourselves."

Mr. Lo tied on his apron and smiled warmly at the girls. "And I thought this was going to be an uneventful day. What can I bring you?"

Zan rubbed her hands together. "Something warm."

"With chocolate," Gwen added. "Lots of chocolate. And those little marshmallows that float around like islands."

"Ah!" Mr. Lo nodded wisely. "An excellent choice. Four Double Hot Chocolate Specials, coming right up."

After he disappeared into the kitchen, Gwen cracked, "Have you ever noticed that everything Hi makes is a Special?"

"I thought you swore off those specials," Rocky said, referring to Gwen's declaration on Saturday.

"I swore off Twinkies," Gwen replied, hopping primly up on the stool. "Besides, that was in a moment of panic. I'm not really responsible for what I said on Saturday. I was scared."

Zan took her usual place on the center stool. "Well, I found out something last night that will make us all scared."

111

"We're all ears," Rocky said as they huddled close to listen.

Zan folded her hands in front of her and said, "After Page and Alice's announcement on Saturday, I decided to do some investigating."

"Like your favorite spy?" Rocky asked. "What's her name?"

"Tiffany Truenote," Zan said. "And she's not a spy, she's a teen detective."

"Well, what did you do?" McGee flipped her chestnut braids over her shoulder and leaned on the counter.

"I went to the studio last night to see if those girls really did drop out of the competition."

"And did they?" Gwen asked.

Zan nodded solemnly. "One even withdrew from her class and switched to another ballet studio."

Rocky whispered softly. "Courtney can sure be vicious."

"You're telling me," Zan agreed.

"What'd you find out?" Gwen demanded. "The suspense is killing me."

Zan reached into the handmade leather purse she'd gotten for Christmas and pulled out a purple writing pad.

"What's that?" Rocky asked.

"Notes," Zan answered. She flipped the pad open to a page marked with a paper clip. Every line was covered in her very neat handwriting.

"You made notes while you were spying?" McGee shook her head in disbelief.

"A good detective always writes everything down." Zan read her notes as if she were reading a police report. "This Saturday, at ten A.M., Miss Alexandra Petrovna will arrive at the Deerfield Academy of Dance. Reporters from all the newspapers will be there."

"Reporters?" Gwen gasped.

Zan nodded. "This is a very big event. Miss Petrovna will hold a news conference which will be televised on all of the major networks."

"TV?" McGee asked. "You mean, camera and lights, and all of that?"

"But that's not the bad part," Zan said. "They're also planning to film the competition."

"Why would they want to do that?" Gwen asked.

"Mrs. Clay talked them into it. I heard her say over the phone that" — Zan consulted her notes — " 'it will be a marvelous way to show the passing of the torch from one generation of ballerinas to another.' "

"Give me a break," Rocky grumbled. "She just wants to get her daughter on TV."

McGee sat up straight. "And that means Mary Bubnik will be on TV, too!"

"Exactly." Zan folded her pad and put it back in her purse and sighed. "Now do you see why I called this meeting?"

Gwen slumped forward on the counter. "Boy, when Mary Bubnik gets up in front of Alexandra Petrovna and that crowd of people, she's going to be laughed right out of the studio."

McGee nodded. "And the whole world will be watching. Geez Louise!"

"Yeah," Rocky mumbled. "And guess who'll be right there with her, looking just as stupid? Us."

"Maybe I'll skip the competition next week," Gwen muttered.

"Presto!" Mr. Lo reappeared with their hot chocolates. "Now what brings you here on such a wintry day?"

"An emergency," Zan replied miserably.

"Umm." Mr. Lo nodded. "I suspected that. Would it have anything to do with my friend, Mary Bubnik?"

McGee narrowed her eyes. "How'd you know?"

Mr. Lo pointed to the fifth stool that sat empty beside them. "She's not here. I hope she's all right."

"She fine," Rocky said. "For now."

"But she's just about to embarrass herself, and humiliate all of us, in front of the entire city of Deerfield," Gwen said.

"And maybe the whole world," McGee groaned.

"How is that possible?" Mr. Lo asked.

"By dancing," McGee explained. "Mary Bubnik is representing us in a competition on Saturday. She's going to dance for the world's greatest ballerina,

114

Alexandra Petrovna. And television cameras will be filming the whole thing."

"Why, that's marvelous!" Mr. Lo said. "Mary must be thrilled."

"She's terribly excited," Zan agreed reluctantly. "She can't wait for Saturday."

"But I don't understand." Mr. Lo scratched his forehead. "How could an honor like that become a source of embarrassment?"

"Mary's the worst dancer in the whole academy," Gwen explained. "She doesn't realize she's going to make a complete fool of herself." She added darkly, "And fools of us, too."

"It's the Bunheads' fault!" Rocky said, hitting her fist in her hand. "They only nominated Mary Bubnik to make sure Courtney Clay would be a shoo-in."

"We can't let this happen," Zan declared.

"I think we should tell Mary everything. Then she'll drop out of the contest."

McGee's words hung in the air heavily. Everyone had been thinking it, but no one had wanted to say it out loud.

"I see," Mr. Lo said. "But wouldn't that hurt her feelings?"

"I'm sure she'll feel just awful," Zan said. "But don't you think embarrassing herself — ?"

"And us," Rocky cut in, "on national TV — "

"Is even worse?" Gwen finished.

"And so your enemies will get what they want without a fight." Mr. Lo stroked his chin thoughtfully. "It's a difficult problem. Do you save face, but in the process hurt a dear friend — or do you support your friend, and risk the chance of being humiliated yourselves?"

"It's awful!" Gwen moaned. "I don't know who I'm madder at — the Bunheads, for nominating Mary, or Mary, for being so blind about what's really going on."

"This reminds me of something I read in a book about battles," Mr. Lo said, taking a seat on his chair behind the counter. "One general had a brilliant strategy that he called 'divide and conquer.'"

"I don't get it," Rocky said.

Zan looked at Mr. Lo with a strange expression on her face. "If our enemy can get us to turn on ourselves," she explained, "then they've won."

"But we're not turning on ourselves," McGee said indignantly.

"We're trying to help Mary," Rocky insisted.

Mr. Lo shrugged his shoulders. "Maybe there are other ways to help her."

"Like how?" Gwen asked as she took a sip of her chocolate.

"Well, what would Mary do if one of you were chosen to be in the competition?"

"She'd be really happy for us," Zan said.

"And even more thrilled that we were going to be on TV," McGee added.

"I see." Mr. Lo picked up a tray of dishes and carried them into the kitchen.

"It wouldn't matter to Mary if we were any good or not," Gwen said slowly.

"What are you getting at?" Rocky asked. She looked completely baffled.

"Mary is our friend," Zan said quietly, "and we should believe in her."

"Like she believes in us," McGee added.

Rocky stared down at her hot chocolate.

"Mary would cheer for any one of us," McGee said, "if we were in the competition."

Rocky nodded. "She wouldn't think twice about it."

Gwen poked at her marshmallows with the tip of her spoon. "Mary's a good friend. She left her practice early last Wednesday, just to help me shop for that dumb bra."

"You know, I don't think winning this contest is what really matters to her," McGee declared.

Rocky kicked at the counter. "We're the ones who've made such a big deal about it."

"That's right," Zan agreed. "I think Mary is just thrilled that she is representing us, and that we think she can do it."

Rocky put her head in her hands. "Boy, do I feel like a jerk!"

"Me, too," Gwen and McGee said in unison.

"And me most of all, for calling this meeting."

Zan stared down at her empty cup. "We should be helping Mary to rehearse, instead of trying to talk her out of it."

"That's right," Rocky said. "Building her confidence."

"You know, my coach says half of winning is thinking like a winner," McGee added, sitting up straight. "We could help Mary think that way and get her all pumped up for the competition."

"Why don't we call her?" Rocky suggested. "I mean, she doesn't live real far away. Maybe she could come join us."

"She'd like that," Zan said.

"Good idea, Rocky," McGee said, her usual energy bouncing back into her voice.

"Should we practice the steps?" Gwen asked. "I would think that would be part of confidence building."

"Most definitely," Zan said.

"Hey, Hi!" McGee called toward the kitchen. "Can we use your phone?"

A hand stuck the receiver through the little pickup window. "I couldn't help overhearing your conversation, and I took the liberty of looking up Mary Bubnik's telephone number."

"Would you dial it for me?" McGee called.

Mr. Lo stuck his head through the window and grinned. "I already have. It's ringing."

118

"Geez Louise!" McGee nearly fell off her stool, fumbling to put the receiver to her ear.

"You know," Zan said, as they waited for Mary to answer, "the only reason we signed up for this ballet class was so we could be together."

"Right." McGee nodded. "*Not* to become great dancers."

Gwen slurped the last of her hot chocolate. "We took this whole thing too seriously."

"And almost broke up our friendship," Rocky said.

"Which is far more important than ballet, or contests, or winning anything," Zan declared.

"Hi, Mary?" McGee called into the receiver. "It's me, McGee."

A little voice, with a familiar southern twang, sounded through the receiver. "McGee! How nice of you to call me."

"Listen, Mary, I was talking to the gang," McGee said, looking at the others. "And we thought maybe you'd like to get together and go over your dance for the competition."

"Why, thank you," came the tinny reply. "When?"

"How does today sound?"

"Oh, gosh, I'd really love to, but it's my big night out with Mom. We go out once a week. Tonight we're having pizza."

"Sounds great."

"Come to think of it, I can't really do anything all week. I have a science project due Friday that I'm working on at school. So, gosh, I don't know what to do."

"Just a minute." McGee put her hand over the receiver and whispered to the group, "Mary can't really practice this week. What should I say?"

"Give me the phone." Rocky hopped up onto the counter and called, "Yo, Mary. It's me, Rocky."

"Hi, Rocky! Where are y'all at?"

"We're down at Hi Lo's." She held up her crossed fingers as she added, "It was really funny, how we just bumped into each other by accident."

"Boy, that is strange," Mary said. "But I was reading in a magazine that that happens all the time — "

"Anyway, we got to talking," Rocky interrupted, before Mary got too far into her story. "And we were all saying how excited we were about your being in the competition. And how we're all behind you, one hundred percent."

Mary Bubnik giggled. "Thanks, Rocky. That means a lot to me."

"Let me talk to her," Gwen said, coming around the side of the counter. She took the receiver and said, "Hi, Mary. I only have one piece of advice. Have a good time on Saturday and afterward I'll treat you to one of Hi Lo's Specials."

"Oooh, Gwen, are you talking about the specials that have chocolate in them?"

"Tons of chocolate." Gwen grinned at the gang.

"Oh, I just can't wait."

Zan stood next to Gwen, putting her ear to one side of the telephone. Rocky and McGee, who were sitting on top of the counter, had their heads together listening on the other side.

"Mary, it's me," Zan breathed.

"Boy, I wish I could be there with y'all," Mary drawled. "It sounds like you're having so much fun."

"We were just practicing a few cheers for you," McGee called.

"That is so sweet." There was a little catch in Mary's voice. She paused for a minute, then spoke again. "I can't tell you how much having y'all as friends means to me. And on Saturday, I'm going to do my very best to make you proud of me."

"We already are," Rocky said in a husky voice.

"So, listen," McGee said, "why don't you come to the studio a little early on Saturday morning, and we'll run over the dance with you. OK?"

"Y'all are going to be there?"

"We wouldn't miss it for the world," Gwen said.

Zan stuck out her hand and the others put theirs on top of it. She declared, "All for one!"

Mary's voice joined them from over the line, "And one for all!"

Chapter Twelve

"Careful!" Mary Bubnik whispered under her breath as she hurried down the icy sidewalk. The freezing weather made each step a potential disaster. Every time she tried to run, her feet would slid out from under her.

Her mother's green Volvo, Mr. Toad, had broken down three blocks from Hillberry Hall.

"I think I forgot to let it warm up," her mother explained, pointing vaguely at the panel of gauges on the dashboard. "So the thingamajig wasn't ready to roll. I think."

They had decided it would take too long to get the car started again, so Mary chose to go the rest of the way on foot. After two blocks she was finally coming up with a system for navigating the slippery concrete.

"Skate. Skate. Walk, walk, walk," she muttered out loud, setting a rhythm for herself. Mary checked the pink-striped watch her father had sent her for Christmas and discovered she was already ten minutes late. She hoped the gang wouldn't be mad at her.

Just thinking about her pals made her smile. The closer the day of the competition had come, her own self-confidence had started to weaken. Their phone call had been just the lift she needed.

Mary spotted a familiar person just in front of her. Even in snow boots she carried herself like a dancer, with perfect posture and her feet turned out. There was no mistaking the commanding way she tilted her chin up in the air.

"Courtney!" Mary cupped her hands around her mouth and yelled, "Hey, Courtney!"

Courtney Clay turned with a big smile on her lips. As soon as she recognized who the caller was, her smile disappeared.

"Yoo-hoo, Courtney," Mary called again, not sure Courtney had seen her. "Wait up, I'll walk with you."

Without a word, Courtney moved to the edge of the sidewalk and trotted along the snowbank. Just as she reached the steps of Hillberry Hall, a cab pulled up to the curb and a woman clad in a long coat with a fur collar and matching cuffs stepped onto the pavement.

"Look out!" Mary Bubnik shouted.

Courtney crashed solidly into the woman's side. The force of the collision threw the woman back against the cab and sent her purse spinning onto the icy sidewalk. The contents spewed out across the snow.

Courtney hesitated for just a moment, then glanced at her watch and gasped. She bolted up the steps of Hillberry Hall and disappeared into the building.

"Are you all right?" Mary asked, rushing up to the woman. The cabdriver had gotten out of the car to see if the lady was injured.

The woman smiled at her sweetly. "I am just a little shaken up, thank you." She picked up her wallet and paid the cabdriver. "Here you are."

"You sure you're OK, lady?" the cabdriver asked. The woman nodded and, once the cab had driven off, bent over to pick up her scattered belongings.

"Here, I'll help you." Mary Bubnik got down on her hands and knees and scooped up several tubes of lipstick, some loose change, a packet of tissues, and a map.

"It's hard to believe that all of this could fit in one small purse." The woman chuckled as they dropped the items into her leather bag.

"Oh, you should see my mom's purse," Mary Bubnik giggled. "It's ten times worse than this. When she's got it really loaded, you could break your wrist carrying it."

When they had finally retrieved everything, the lady stood up and turned in a slow, elegant circle, carefully inspecting the building around her.

Mary watched, mesmerized. The stranger wore a tall fur hat that matched her coat. She had a long, straight nose and high cheekbones. Her skin was so pale that Mary wondered if she had ever been out in the sun at all. The deep red lipstick and red rouge made her look even more exotic, like a model in a magazine.

"I was looking for a place to get a cup of hot tea," the woman said as she put on a pair of dark sunglasses.

"I know the perfect place," Mary said. "My friend, Hi Lo, owns it."

"Hi Lo?" the lady repeated with a smile.

"Isn't his name wonderful?" Mary grinned. "He's Chinese."

"I see. And what is your name?"

"Mary Bubnik."

"Well, Mary Bubnik," the woman said, her lips parting in a big, beautiful smile. "May I buy you a soft drink?"

Mary didn't know what to say. Her friends were waiting in the studio to help her rehearse. On the other hand, the lady was being so nice and Mary didn't want to seem rude.

"Well, OK," she replied. "But I have to hurry."

"I understand." The woman patted Mary on the

arm. "It's the least I can do to thank you for helping me."

"Oh, it was nothing." Mary kicked at the snowbank shyly. "Anybody would have done the same."

"That other girl didn't," the woman reminded her. "She didn't even stop to see if I was all right."

Mary thought of the competition and said, "That girl has a lot on her mind just now." Mary led them both across the street to Hi Lo's. "You see, Courtney wants to be a ballerina someday."

"A ballerina?" The lady raised an eyebrow. "And is that what you want to be?"

"Me?" Mary Bubnik laughed. "I could never be one. Ballerinas are beautiful, like birds or butterflies. You know, so delicate and light." She grimaced. "I am a major klutz. I mean, I can hardly walk without tripping over my feet."

The lady smiled gently.

At the front of the tiny restaurant Mary announced, "Here we are!" Then she threw open the door and sang out, "Hi, Hi!"

McGee checked her watch for the twentieth time, then continued pacing back and forth on their side of the dressing room. Finally she declared, "Well, I think we may have overdone it with ol' Mary Bubnik."

"What do you mean?" Gwen called from behind the mirror. She was changing into her leotard and a black sweatshirt. Mrs. Hays had called the academy to see if Gwen could wear a sweatshirt until she got used to her bra. They had agreed, just so long as it was the regulation black.

"I think we made her so confident that she didn't even think she had to rehearse," McGee explained.

"Don't you think it might be something completely different?" Zan asked.

"Like what?" Rocky demanded, pulling her frizzy hair into a ponytail on the side of her head.

"Maybe Mary Bubnik got scared."

"Scared of what?" Rocky asked.

"Losing," a new voice announced from the curtained doorway. They all turned to see Courtney Clay step into the room. She strolled confidently over to the dressing table and removed her coat.

She was already dressed for the audition. Courtney had French-braided her hair into a lovely ponytail at her neck. Woven into the braid was a thin pink satin ribbon. Her leotard and tights were brand-new and a tiny gold chain with a little ballerina dangling from it circled her neck.

It made Gwen depressed just to look at her.

The curtain rustled and Page and Alice walked in. They both cried, "Oooh, Courtney, you look fantastic."

"Thank you." Courtney nodded her head like a queen accepting a compliment. "Mother and I discussed whether I should wear the gold necklace for the audition or save it for the moment I present the flowers to Alexandra." She smiled smugly and said, "We decided I should wear it both times."

"Wait a minute," Rocky protested. "You act like you've got this in the bag."

"Don't I?"

"Well, like my coach always says," McGee said, "it ain't over till it's over."

"It looks pretty over to us." Page gestured to the room. "I mean, Mary Bubnik didn't even bother to show up."

"She'll be here," Rocky grumbled.

"Before or after the audition?" Courtney asked sweetly. She stood up and, clasping one foot with her hand, extended it straight out in front of her. Then she rotated her leg out to the side and pulled it up almost to her ear.

"If you're not careful," Gwen teased, "you could get stuck like that."

"Very funny," Alice Wescott said. "I'd like to see you try it."

"Not a chance." Gwen sat down on the wooden bench and dug into her blue canvas bag. "Something might snap. Human beings were only meant to touch their toes. And maybe do a few sit-ups." She pulled out a bag of M&Ms and passed them around to the gang.

"If you keep eating that junk," Courtney said, "you

won't be able to *see* your toes, let alone touch them."

Gwen paused in mid-bite, trying to think of a comeback. Her mind went blank.

"Maybe we should tell Alexandra Petrovna about your fear of the dark," Rocky said scornfully. "I mean, the lights might go out on the stage and there you'd be — crying and calling for your mother."

Courtney's nostrils flared. "You're just upset because your friend got cold feet and didn't show up." She smiled triumphantly. "And I'm going to win."

"That's not true," Rocky shot back, gritting her teeth.

Courtney strode to the curtain, then turned and asked, "Isn't it?"

Alice and Page followed their leader out of the room without another look at the gang.

Rocky hit her fist in her hand. "Courtney's right. I *hate* it when she's right."

"I just can't believe that Mary Bubnik would do this," Zan said, shaking her head. "She knows how important this is. I really think something terrible might have happened to her."

McGee's eyes widened. "Like a car accident, or something?"

Zan nodded slowly.

"Let's call her mother."

Zan shook her head. "Her mother would have

129

been driving. The first thing a detective would do is call the hospitals and then the police."

"Police!" Gwen yelped. "Why should we call them? She hasn't committed any crime."

"But she might have been a victim," Rocky cut in. Since her dad was a security policeman on the air base, she knew a lot about standard police procedures. "They'd be able to follow up on any kidnapping suspicions, a possible hostage situation — "

"Hostage?" Gwen and McGee cried out at the same time.

Rocky nodded grimly.

"Geez Louise!" McGee exclaimed. "This is getting serious!"

"Poor Mary," Zan said. "I truly hope she's OK."

"I'm just fine," Mary said, throwing back the curtain to the dressing room.

Gwen leaped to her feet. "You're alive!"

"We were so worried about you," Zan said as she gave her a big hug.

"What happened?" Rocky asked as they crowded around Mary. "Was it your car?"

Mary Bubnik nodded.

"I knew it," McGee said, shaking her head. "How bad was the accident?"

"Was anybody hurt?" Gwen asked. "Is your mom OK?"

"Mom's fine, she's waiting a few blocks away,"

Mary replied. "Something about the thingamajig not getting a chance to warm up."

Gwen looked puzzled. "What kind of an accident is that?"

"There wasn't any accident," Mary Bubnik said. "Unless you count Courtney running into that lady on the street."

"Wait a minute," Rocky interrupted. "If there wasn't an accident, and you and your mom are both OK, then why were you late?"

"Well, it's like this," Mary began. "I was over at Hi Lo's having a Coke — "

"You *what?*" they shouted together.

Mary nodded and took off her coat. "Courtney knocked over this woman and — "

"I cannot believe you," Rocky broke in, her voice quivering with outrage. "Here we got here early to help you rehearse."

"And build up your confidence," McGee chimed in. "Just so you could face this audition in a winning state of mind."

"Then when you didn't show," Zan went on, "we were terrified that you'd been in an accident."

"Or kidnapped," Rocky added.

"Or murdered," McGee said.

"Or worse," Gwen finished.

Rocky put her hands on her hips. "Now you won't have a chance to prepare for your audition in front of the greatest ballerina in the whole world."

"Doesn't that mean anything to you?" Gwen added.

Mary shrugged helplessly. "I've practiced all week long. I guess I'm about as good as I'll ever get."

"There you are!" Miss Delacorte stuck her head through the curtain. She called over her shoulder, "Mary Bubnik has arrived." Then she turned back to the girls and lowered her voice. "I was so afraid that Courtney would be the only contestant. At least, now it will look like a fair contest."

"*Look* like one?" Zan repeated.

"Did I say that?" Miss Delacorte fluttered her hands nervously. "I meant, it will *be* a fair contest. Anyway, it's time for the audition to begin."

Mary Bubnik quickly took off her parka and snow boots. She was already wearing her leotard and tights under her clothes. The tights sagged in little wrinkles around her knees and ankles. One sleeve of her leotard had crept up to her elbow while the other was still at her wrist. Everything about her looked off center. Even her curly hair had flattened where she'd worn her stocking cap. The rest stuck out in tight curls around her ears.

"I'm ready," Mary called cheerfully. "Wish me luck!"

The gang watched Mary Bubnik stumble over the doorsill as she left the dressing room and answered glumly, "Good luck."

Chapter Thirteen

"What are all these people doing here?" Mary Bubnik stood frozen at the door of the studio.

The room was jammed with dancers and students from every other class in the academy. People were lined up three deep along the mirrored walls. Photographers clustered around the studio entrance and a television crew had trained a set of blinding lights on the doorway.

"They've just dropped by to meet the famous ballerina," Gwen said, trying her best to sound casual.

"And maybe watch the audition," Rocky mumbled out the side of her mouth.

"Oh." Mary Bubnik swallowed hard.

"It's no big deal," McGee added, thumping Mary on the back. "Really."

A little platform with chairs on it had been set up near the piano. Annie Springer was placing a red rose on the middle chair. She was dressed in a simple black dress with elegant high heels. The touch of extra makeup made her look prettier than ever.

In the far corner of the room, Courtney Clay was warming up, doing *pliés* and stretches at the *barre*. Although her expression seemed calm and impassive, it was clear by her uneven movements that she was nervous, too. Page and Alice hovered by her side.

Mary Bubnik stared at the room full of people with glazed eyes.

"Don't you think you should warm up?" McGee whispered to Mary Bubnik.

"OK," Mary answered. Her eyes were two huge pools of blue in her pale face. "But what should I do?"

"Try a few of those *pliés*." Gwen pointed to Courtney, who was standing with her heels together in first position. She slowly bent her knees, then straightened back up to a standing position.

Mary moved swiftly toward the *barre*. She grasped the rail with her right hand and, like a robot, bobbed up and down five times. Rocky grimaced at how awkward she looked.

"Maybe you should just practice the steps to your dance," Zan suggested.

"OK." Mary Bubnik stepped away from the *barre*. She squeezed her eyes shut and held her breath. Then her eyes popped open wide with horror. "Oh, no!"

"What?" Zan asked.

"Y'all aren't going to believe this, but I can't remember the first step."

"I believe it," Gwen muttered under her breath.

Mary Bubnik turned to Zan desperately. "It's gone completely out of my head."

"Geez Louise!" McGee groaned. "This could be a total disaster."

"Mary, you're just a little nervous," Zan said gently. "Remember, we're all on your side." She shot McGee a warning look.

"Oh, yeah, we're behind you," McGee said quickly, "one hundred percent." She mustered a smile that she hoped looked encouraging.

Across the room Courtney was going over a few of her steps on the floor. Zan asked, "Do any of those steps look familiar?"

"That's it! That's our dance." Mary Bubnik watched Courtney a few seconds, then mimicked her movements. "Thanks, Zan," Mary whispered as she practiced a little crossover step called a *pas de bourrée*. "I guess I am a little nervous."

Suddenly there was a loud commotion from the front office.

"Darlings, it is so good to see you!" a lilting voice carried into the studio from the reception area. "You both look fabulous."

"So do you," Mr. Anton's voice replied cheerfully. "Younger than ever."

Then Miss Jo's voice could be heard. "Alexandra, Alexandra, how do you do it?"

"All work and no play," the woman's voice answered with a pleasant laugh. "I haven't seen the sun in years."

"Come meet my dancers," Mr. Anton announced. "Ever since they heard you were coming, they've talked of nothing else."

Everyone in the studio stood at attention, all eyes trained on the door waiting for the moment when they would finally see the great dancer in the flesh.

Alexandra Petrovna swept into the room, followed by the directors of the academy. Lightbulbs popped and there was a loud whirring from dozens of cameras. Several of the dancers burst into applause, giving her a rousing ovation.

"My, my, my!" the elegant woman exclaimed. She clasped her hands in front of her throat and laughed delightedly. "What a lovely welcome." She made a beautiful sweeping curtsy to the room. "Thank you all so very much."

This set off a whole new round of cheering and clapping.

Alexandra Petrovna glided around the room, greeting each dancer, who curtsied respectfully as she passed.

Zan watched Miss Petrovna's every movement in fascination. She carried herself so regally that Zan found it hard to imagine her making a daring escape hidden in a suitcase. It was as if a magical, rare creature, like a unicorn, had suddenly appeared.

Gwen tugged at her black sweatshirt wishing she hadn't worn it. If she had worn only her leotard, she might have looked more like a dancer.

As she passed Courtney Clay, Miss Petrovna paused for a long moment with a puzzled look on her face. The red rushed into Courtney's face so fast that her cheeks glowed. She dropped her head and stared hard at the floor until Miss Petrovna moved on to the next student.

Zan, Rocky, and McGee curtsied as best they could when Miss Petrovna passed them. Gwen hid behind them, hoping no one would notice her sweatshirt.

The sight of the dancer brought Mary Bubnik out of her daze. "*You're* Alexandra Petrovna, the famous ballerina?"

Miss Petrovna nodded. Rocky and the others

could hardly believe their ears. No one else, not even the members of the professional company, had dared to actually speak to Alexandra Petrovna. Gwen tried to stomp on Mary's toes to get her to be quiet.

"I can't believe it!" Mary rattled on. "Wait'll I tell my mother. She will just keel over and die!"

Miss Petrovna smiled sweetly and moved along.

Mr. Anton made a brief speech of welcome on behalf of the Deerfield Ballet. The mayor of Deerfield presented Miss Petrovna with a key to the city. There was more cheering from the crowd, and then Mr. Anton raised his arms for silence.

"Miss Petrovna is here to select the young girl to present flowers to her after tomorrow night's performance," he announced. "Of course, it is a great honor. We have two dancers from the middle grades, chosen by their peers, who will dance for the prima ballerina. They are" — he consulted a sheet of paper in his hand — "Courtney Clay..."

A round of applause came from Courtney's side of the room as she moved across the wooden floor to the center of the room.

"... and Mary Bubnik."

The gang applauded as loudly as they could. Rocky gave the thumbs-up sign as McGee whistled.

Mary Bubnik looked at her friends and smiled. Then she turned and promptly stumbled over her floppy ballet shoes.

"Wait, Mary, wait!" McGee shouted. Mary looked

back to see McGee pulling off her own dance shoes and gesturing for Mary to put them on. Rocky and Gwen got the idea and, dropping to the floor, removed Mary's shoes.

Moments later Mary Bubnik stood in fifth position, facing Miss Alexandra Petrovna.

Courtney Clay looked poised and confident, holding her arms in a beautiful oval by her side. She tilted her chin up toward the ceiling, looking every inch the ballerina she was determined to become some day.

Mary was the complete opposite. Her arms hung stiffly at her sides. She fidgeted slightly as she tried to blow a strand of hair out of her eyes.

"The audition will begin," Mr. Anton announced.

The room fell silent. Mrs. Bruce played the short introduction on the piano and Mary caught Miss Petrovna's eye. She waved gaily at the ballerina and then began her first step.

McGee groaned out loud. Gwen buried her face in Rocky's thick mane of hair and shook her head.

The two girls danced together as the music played. Courtney was a model of concentration, performing each step with precision.

"Courtney's got it in the bag," Rocky whispered to Zan.

"I'm afraid she does," Zan replied. "But Mary's doing awfully well."

It was true. Mary obviously didn't have Courtney's

139

skill, but she made up for it with the bouncy energy she brought to her steps.

"Hey Gwen," McGee whispered, "maybe you should watch this."

With each step Mary danced with more confidence. Her radiant smile grew brighter and brighter.

"You can say one thing about her," McGee observed. "She sure looks happy."

"That's 'cause she doesn't know she's losing," Gwen said.

"I think she's smiling because she's really having fun," Zan said.

Mary went blank right in the middle of the next combination. A quick glance at Courtney's feet and she found her place again. She went on to the next step without hesitation.

"Atta girl!" Rocky declared.

The music came to an end and the two dancers finished in front of the platform. Courtney swept down low in an elaborate bow.

"Come on, Mary," Zan urged under her breath. "Don't forget your curtsy."

Annie caught Mary's eye and made a little gesture with her hand while mouthing the word "Bow!"

With a start Mary remembered and bobbed up and down in a short little curtsy, then hurried to join her friends.

"Did I do OK?" she asked, her face bright with excitement.

"OK?" Rocky replied, lightly punching her on the shoulder. "You were hot!"

"I didn't want to let y'all down." Mary's words tumbled out in a rush.

"You danced your absolute best," Gwen said.

"And you can't ask for anything more than that," McGee added.

"We're so proud of you," Zan whispered, squeezing Mary's hand.

Mr. Anton clapped his hands for silence and the crowd settled down. "Miss Petrovna will now select her flower bearer."

Courtney strode confidently up to the platform, wearing the look of a winner. Mary joined her and waited nervously for the famous ballerina to make her decision.

Miss Petrovna stood up from her seat and cleared her throat.

"First, I must say," she began, nodding at the two girls, "thank you both."

She looked around the crowded studio and a smile crept over her face.

"As I stand here, so many memories come back to me — of when I, too, was a young student of the dance." She shook her head slowly. "I have spent most of my life in rooms like this, all over the world."

Her voice resonated around the quiet studio. No one dared breathe for fear of interrupting her.

"The life of a dancer can be very lonely. It is so

important that we always remember to be kind to our fellow artists and help them whenever we can. Because, after the lights of the theatre grow dim, and the applause of the crowd fades away, we dancers have only each other."

She looked at Courtney and smiled. "Miss Clay, you are a lovely dancer. Your technique is superb for one so young. I am sure that, in time, you will find your place in the ballet."

Courtney seemed to swell with pride at each compliment.

"But to do the steps correctly is not enough," Miss Petrovna continued. "One must have an unselfish, generous heart. That is where the soul of the ballet lives and breathes."

Courtney looked confused and glanced uncertainly over her shoulder at her mother.

"A beautiful heart makes a beautiful dancer. That is why I select a young dancer who makes up in spirit what she lacks in ability. I choose a girl who understands that one act of kindness is worth a thousand perfect pirouettes. I choose Mary Bubnik!"

There was a stunned silence as everyone in the room turned to stare. Mary Bubnik stood still, her jaw hanging open in amazement. Finally she stammered, "Y-you mean, me?"

Miss Petrovna smiled and nodded her head. "Yes you, my little friend."

Mary jumped up and down, squealing, "I don't

believe it! Me? Wait till my mom hears about this! Just wait!"

McGee and the others ran over to Mary and almost knocked her off her feet with hugs of congratulations. Miss Petrovna took the rose that had been placed on her chair and handed it to Mary Bubnik, who cradled it in her arms.

"This is the most wonderful day of my entire life," Mary declared.

"I am so glad," the ballerina replied.

"Miss Petrovna, these are the girls I was telling you about — my very best friends in the whole wide world." Mary beamed at her friends, adding, "I couldn't have done it without them."

"Is that so?" Miss Petrovna said. "Then perhaps they would like to join you backstage as my guests, and watch the performance from the wings?"

"What?" a familiar voice gasped indignantly behind them. "Mother, that's not fair."

"Hold it!" a photographer shouted. Mary Bubnik and the gang turned to beam at the camera. They were grinning so hard their faces hurt.

Chapter Fourteen

"Look, you guys, we made the *Deerfield Times*!" Mary Bubnik waved the newspaper over her head as she ran to join her friends by the stage door of Patterson Auditorium.

Rocky held up five newspapers of her own. "Our neighbors came over this evening and gave us these." She grinned happily. "Boy, was my dad proud!"

"Geez Louise," McGee chuckled as she stared at the photograph on the front page. "We're celebrities."

"Let me look at that picture one more time." Gwen took the clipping out of Mary's hand.

The picture showed Miss Petrovna standing behind Mary with her hands on the girl's shoulders. Rocky, Gwen, and Zan stood on either side, beaming from ear to ear. McGee was giving the camera the "thumbs-up" sign. A crowd of onlookers filled the background, smiling happily — except for one.

"Look at Courtney's face." Rocky pointed to the image of a dark-haired girl glaring at the camera with her arms crossed. "She sure looks mad!"

"And I sure feel scared!" Mary giggled nervously. "I wish I didn't have to wear this dress. It itches everywhere."

Mary's mother had bought her a special green velvet dress for the occasion. She wore white tights and black patent leather pumps. On top of her blonde curls perched a crooked green velvet bow.

"Just be glad you're not wearing a *you-know-what*," Gwen grumbled. "Every time I raise my arm the thing rides up around my neck. It's just awful!"

"I know," Rocky said with a sly grin.

"How would you know?" Gwen tugged at the elastic around her rib cage, then folded her arms.

"Should we show her?" Zan asked the others.

"It was supposed to be a surprise for later," Mary said with a giggle. "But I can't wait."

"OK, here goes." McGee counted out loud, "One, two . . ."

"Three!" All four girls pulled down the shoulders of their outfits, revealing matching white cotton bra straps.

145

Gwen gasped in surprise. "Are you guys wearing what I think you're wearing?"

"You got it!" Rocky grinned. "We didn't want you to feel alone."

"And now the Bunheads are outnumbered," Zan announced with glee.

"Next thing you know," Mary added, "they'll be out buying bras, trying to keep up with us."

"Gosh, you guys," Gwen mumbled, "I don't know what to say."

"Hey!" Rocky shrugged. "It's no big deal."

McGee draped her arm over Gwen's shoulder. "Yeah, we're friends, right?"

"We must be." Gwen's voice quivered. "Because only true friends would ever put up with this kind of torture."

"Mary Bubnik?"

Mary looked up to see a dark-haired woman dressed in an apron standing beside her. She was carrying a long pink tutu with brightly colored ribbons laced on the bodice.

"Yes, that's me," Mary replied.

"And these are your friends?" the woman asked, with a nod to the gang. "Please, you will come with me."

The girls hesitated for a moment and the woman laughed pleasantly. "It is all right. I am Madame Petrovna's dresser, Nicole. She would like to see you."

The girls scrambled to their feet and hurried after

Nicole down the corridor. The woman stopped outside one of the dressing rooms and tapped on the door lightly. "Madame?"

"Entrez!" a voice called from within. "Come in!"

Nicole turned to the girls and said, "Madame will see you now, but don't linger. She must prepare for this evening's performance."

The door was slightly ajar, and Mary Bubnik pushed it open the rest of the way.

"Is that you, my little friend?" Alexandra Petrovna called. "Come in! Come in!"

The ballerina was seated at her dressing table, wearing a pale blue and white kimono. She applied the last of her eyeliner and smiled at them in the mirror. "I wanted to see you girls now, before the ballet begins, because I won't be able to talk to you during the performance." She picked up a powder puff, dabbed it on her wrist, then lightly patted her face. "The role of *Giselle* takes all of my concentration."

"We know you're going to be just perfect," Mary said earnestly.

Miss Petrovna laughed. "Thank you, my dear. I hope I do not disappoint you."

"Never!" Rocky and McGee exclaimed.

The ballerina smoothed her hair, then turned around to face them. She was already wearing her pink tights and a pair of beautiful satin toe shoes.

147

"Your shoes look brand-new!" Mary Bubnik exclaimed.

The dancer extended her leg out in a beautifully arched point. "They are. They are handsewn for me by a wonderful cobbler in Paris. I wear out one pair a performance."

"Every night?" McGee blinked in amazement.

"That is right."

"Boy, this *Giselle* part must be hard!" Rocky shook her head in awe. "I've had the same ballet shoes for two years, and they've *never* worn out."

Miss Petrovna clasped her hands together in delight. Her laughter bubbled up out of her throat like notes from a musical instrument. "I am so glad I met you girls. It has been a real treat!"

There was a light knock at the door. The dark-haired woman entered the room, carrying another costume, and said, "Fifteen minutes to places, Madame."

"Oh, I am so sorry," Miss Petrovna said with a sigh, "but now you must leave me, and take your places backstage."

Mary Bubnik and the others backed slowly toward the door. They couldn't take their eyes off the beautiful ballerina.

"Before you go, I'll let you in on a little secret." The ballerina whispered, "The best way to watch a ballet is not with your eyes — but with your heart."

"With our hearts," Zan murmured.

"That is right." The ballerina turned back to face her reflection in the mirror. "*Au revoir, mes enfants!* Good-bye, for now the ballet is about to begin."

The stage manager, a short balding man with glasses, led them backstage to a space in the wings where five chairs had been placed. He took his position on the tall stool next to the lighting control board and put on a headset. Soon they could hear him murmuring instructions to other technicians in the theatre.

In the dim light of backstage, dancers, wearing legwarmers and sweaters over their costumes, warmed up all around them. The dancers held on to pieces of scenery and did exercises to stretch their muscles.

"Hey!" Mary pointed to one dancer doing *pliés* and whispered, "We do that in our class."

Zan nodded. "All dancers do those exercises before every performance."

"Places, everyone!" the stage manager called to the dancers in the wings. The girls watched in awe as one beautiful dancer after another took their starting position behind the curtain. The dancers were dressed like people from a peasant village, in gaily colored costumes. The men wore boots and carried bows and arrows as if they'd just been hunting.

The orchestra began the overture, and the girls held their breaths as the big red curtain slowly lifted.

The lights on the stage brightened, and they were transported into a make-believe world.

When Alexandra Petrovna first stepped onto the stage, the auditorium exploded into loud applause. The girls wanted to join in, but the stage manager put his finger to his lips, instructing them to keep silent.

The next two hours passed like a dream. Rocky was the first to cry when Giselle died and soon the rest of the gang joined her, sniffling and passing around a Kleenex that Zan had tucked in her purse.

When Giselle became a spirit in the fairy world Alexandra seemed to float through the air across the stage. Zan sat with her hands clasped in front of her, murmuring, "She's truly the most beautiful dancer in the world."

"In the universe!" McGee said.

Before they knew it, the stage manager was giving directions over his headset and the big red velvet curtain came down across the stage. Applause filled the huge auditorium.

The backstage was suddenly crowded with ballerinas in white tutus lining up to take their bows. Their faces were all covered with beads of sweat.

The beautiful Alexandra Petrovna was met in the wings by two assistants. One draped a towel around her neck and the other handed her a glass of water. Her eyes were shining as she focused her entire attention on the stage.

The stage manager pushed several buttons and then whispered to Mary, "Stand over there, and I'll give you the signal to go."

"But I don't have the flowers," Mary Bubnik hissed in a sudden panic.

"Don't worry, they'll be here," the stage manager replied. "Curtain up!" he barked into his headset and row upon row of dancers ran onto the stage to take their bows.

"Relax, Mary," Rocky said as the gang gathered around her. "This will be a piece of cake."

McGee pointed to the center of the stage and whispered, "You just walk straight out there — "

"On your toes," Zan reminded her. "With your chin held high."

"And then hand Miss Petrovna the bouquet," Gwen finished. "Easy."

An usher in a maroon jacket suddenly appeared out of the darkness. He held a huge bouquet of red roses tied together with a big white bow. He lay them in Mary Bubnik's arms and disappeared. The bouquet was so large that the others could barely see Mary's blonde curls peeking out over the top.

"Stand by," the stage manager whispered.

Mary nodded. Her mouth suddenly went dry and the sound of the applause was muffled by the sound of her own heart pounding in her chest.

Alexandra Petrovna floated onto the stage and curtsied gracefully all the way to the floor. The audience leaped to its feet, and shouts of "Bravo!" rang through the air. She curtsied to her partner, then gestured for the *corps de ballet* to take another bow.

The applause grew louder and louder.

"I think I am going to pass out," Mary murmured as the stage began to spin in front of her eyes. "I'll never be able to do it."

Then her whole body went stiff for a moment. Just as quickly, she relaxed. The gang heard her murmur, "Thanks."

"For what?" Rocky asked.

"For holding my hand."

The stage manager shouted, "Go!" and Mary tiptoed into the light.

"*I* didn't hold her hand," Rocky said to the group. "Did any of you guys?"

Everyone slowly shook their head.

"Then who...?" Rocky suddenly gasped. "You don't think?"

McGee held up one hand. "Listen!"

They cocked their heads. The sound was faint, but they all heard it.

Thunk. Drag. Thunk. Drag.

"Ivan Scapinskeeeeeeeeey!"

As Mary Bubnik approached the ballerina, a group of four terrified girls suddenly appeared on the stage behind her. They clung to each other tightly, staring wide-eyed off into the wings.

152

Mary handed Miss Petrovna the bouquet, remembering to do her curtsy. She only wobbled once, when she spotted her friends clustered behind her. Her face broke into a huge grin, and she stepped back to join them.

"Thanks for coming, guys," she whispered out of the corner of her mouth.

"We couldn't let you go it alone," Rocky answered. "We thought you might be scared." She glanced nervously over her shoulder toward the wings.

As Miss Alexandra Petrovna took her final bow, Mary Bubnik and the gang linked arms and walked offstage.

"I suppose it's possible to be happier than this," Mary said, beaming at her friends, "but I'm not sure how."

WIN A BAD NEWS BALLET SWEATSHIRT

Enter the

Bad News Ballet
C O N T E S T !

Rocky, Zan, Mary Bubnik, Gwen, and McGee may not like to dance…but they sure can make you laugh! To them, ballet is *bad news*!

100 Winners!

But here's *great news* for you! You can win your very own Bad News Ballet sweatshirt. It's easy to enter the Bad News Ballet contest! Just complete the coupon below and return by August 31, 1989.

This fabulous big, oversized sweatshirt is pink with the Bad News Ballet logo on front! One size fits all! Wear it to your next dance rehearsal—or just for fun!

Rules: Entries must be postmarked by August 31, 1989. Contestants must be between the ages of 7 and 12. The winner will be picked at random from all eligible entries received. No purchase necessary. Valid only in the U.S.A. Employees of Scholastic Inc., affiliates, subsidiaries, and their families not eligible. Void where prohibited. The winner will be notified by mail.

Fill in your name, age, and address below or write the information on a 3" × 5" piece of paper and mail to:
THE BAD NEWS BALLET CONTEST, Scholastic Inc., Dept BNB, 730 Broadway, New York, NY 10003.

- -

The Bad News Ballet Sweatshirt Contest

Where did you get this book?

☐ Bookstore ☐ Drug Store ☐ Supermarket
☐ Discount Store ☐ Book Club ☐ Book Fair
☐ Other _____
                              specify

Name _____

Birthday _____ Age _____

Street _____

City, State, Zip _____

BNB1088